Ghoul You Be My Valentine

Ghoul You Be My Valentine

A Ravenmist Whodunit
Book Two

BY OLIVIA JAYMES

www.OliviaJaymes.com

Ghoul You Be My Valentine?

It's time for another Ravenmist Whodunit! A tiny Midwestern town with charming covered bridges, quirky residents, delightful antique shops, and more than their share of haunted activity.

Tedi has another packed inn of people for the Ravenmist Valentine's Day Ball. The evening was a complete success until she and Jack find a dead body on the back patio with a Cupid's arrow through his heart. There's no shortage of suspects for his murder either. Jack will have his hands full paring down the list.

And Tedi? She's staying out of this. No way is she going to be pulled into it. Not after last time. She has her own investigation. She and her friend Missy are trying to find why the town has suddenly been infused with paranormal energy. Ghosts are literally getting up and dancing around. It's all going well too. That is until the investigation starts to hit just a little bit too close to home.

Hop into your ghostmobile and take a ride with Tedi as she meets a spirit who doesn't think he's dead, two ghosts in love, and a hard partying specter who just might have witnessed the murder. It's a hauntingly good time in the little town of Ravenmist and you're invited to the party.

Chapter One

IT WAS CHICKEN and dumplings day at Daisy's diner, The Grateful Raven. The perfect cold weather comfort food, and I was digging into my bowl as if I hadn't eaten in days. The chicken was tasty, the gravy perfectly seasoned, and the dumplings were tender. I don't know what witchcraft Daisy used to make this dish, but I had never been able to replicate it and I can assure you I've tried many times.

Excuse me, I haven't introduced myself. I'm Theodosia "Tedi" Hamilton and I own Ravenmist Inn, a rambling old Victorian that's been in my father's family for generations. The entire property consists of several acres and six painstakingly maintained buildings. I'm also the president of the local paranormal society, which I guess makes me a ghost hunter. I've now met a few spirits though, so I wouldn't say that I was hunting anymore. Oh, and my best friend Missy is the Grim Reaper. And the owner of the local bookstore.

Hmmmm…I think you're all caught up. Nice to meet you and glad you could stop by. Have a bowl of Daisy's chicken and dumplings or maybe the pot roast. They're both melt in your mouth. Don't leave Ravenmist without trying the apple pie.

My dining companion, Sheriff Jack Garrett, smacked his lips and made a yummy sound, which was kind of funny coming from a man his size. "I admit it. Food does taste better here than in Chicago."

"Told you," I said, shoving another dumpling in my mouth. "She has some secret ingredient that she won't disclose."

"Love?" Jack smirked. We were eating lunch together in our effort to become *friends*. It was going...fine. We still didn't agree on a great deal of subjects, but we had managed to find some common ground.

Strange how the topic of seeing ghosts was one that we still didn't concur on, considering only about three months ago Jack had seen a ghost in my office. He hadn't mentioned it then and he still hadn't now. At first, I'd thought it was because he didn't see Terrence – the ghost that haunted my clothes closet – but now I think it's because Jack doesn't like to be wrong. He's stubborn that way.

"I was thinking it might be wild garlic, but we can go with love," I replied with my own smirk. "Especially as the Valentine Ball is tonight. Love is definitely in the air."

Except for me, which I was fine with, by the way. I'd been married, and I had sort of a "been there, done that, worn the t-shirt" attitude about love. Last I heard my ex was going through women in the Greater Chicago area like a lawnmower. More power to him as long as I didn't have to be around.

Jack's gaze ran over the cheesy pink and red decorations

stuck to every flat surface and grimaced. "Everywhere. It's not even a real holiday. It's made up by corporations to guilt men into buying cards, candy, and flowers."

"Don't forget jewelry."

The sheriff had been married at one point in his life and he had a teenage son named Tyler, but he'd never said a single word about his past relationship, not even her name. He could have been divorced or widowed – the town didn't have a clue – but he was as cynical about romance as I was.

Jack snorted. "Of course, jewelry. How could I forget? Roses and chocolates aren't enough anymore. If we really love someone, we're supposed to blow a wad of cash on a ring or a necklace."

"Or a romantic weekend at an old Victorian Inn."

"I suppose you're booked solid."

I took the last bite of my lunch and pushed my empty plate away, patting my full stomach.

"I've been completely booked for this weekend since before Labor Day."

"The ball is that big of a draw? You do throw a hell of a party."

And it just about killed Jack to admit it. I could see it in his expression.

"I do, but that's not why they're coming to town. They want to try and see the Young Lovers."

His brows pinched together, and he shook his head. "The Young Lovers?"

3

"You've been in town almost a year and haven't heard the story?"

"The story? Humor me."

It was so cheesy I knew he'd hate it.

"Supposedly a young couple drowned in Raven Lake over a hundred years ago because their parents didn't want them to get married. So they ran away together, held hands, and jumped into the icy lake swearing that no one could separate them. Now people say that if a couple throws a flower into the lake on Valentine's Day they will be blessed with eternal love and happiness."

A smiling Daisy slapped the lunch check onto the table. "That's what we're planning to do."

"What are you planning to do?" Jack asked, grabbing at the check before I could get it. We were always jockeying to be the one to pick up the tab and he had faster reflexes.

"Throw a flower into the lake," Daisy explained. "The stories are true. I've seen it work."

I'd also seen it not work. My own parents had told me and my sisters the story of how they'd thrown their own flower into Raven Lake when they were dating. It might have worked for awhile but it was not *eternal*. They were currently getting a divorce.

"I didn't realize things were that serious between you and Colin," I said, giving Jack a kick under the table. He'd opened his mouth to say something negative and Daisy didn't need to hear it. If I could keep my opinions to myself, he could, too.

Daisy's brows shot up and she started to laugh. "Colin and I broke up right after New Year's. I've barely thought about him. No, I'm seeing Gavin now. Gavin Baldwin."

Gavin Baldwin owned a dairy farm outside of town and made artisanal cheeses as a hobby. If Daisy was dating him, I expected to see an inventive macaroni and cheese dish on the menu very soon.

"That's...fast," Jack said. "Are you sure he's the one?"

I gave our sheriff another kick under the table and he scowled at me in return.

Daisy beamed, her face glowing like a woman in love. "I'm very sure. When you know, you know. We're going to go to the ball tonight and then around midnight go out to the lake. Gavin is such a romantic. Passionate, too."

Whoa. I wasn't ready to hear any girlish confessions about Daisy and Gavin. Jack had a peculiar look on his face as well, like his stomach was queasy.

"I'm really happy for you, Daisy."

And I was. Better her than me. I nudged Jack with my foot. Again. This was becoming tiresome. Could he just get the hint already?

"Me too," he said with a smile that wasn't quite genuine, but luckily Daisy was too in love to notice.

Jack dropped a few bills onto the check. "The meal was fantastic as always, Daisy, but I do need to get back to work."

I tried to pull out a twenty and hand it to him, but he gave me a nasty look. Sighing, I stuffed it back into my purse.

"I'll get lunch next time."

"Sounds good." He checked his watch. "I'll come by about two in the afternoon to check your decorations for any major hazards."

Oh goody. I was so looking forward to that. Not.

"This isn't Halloween or even Christmas. There's nothing for you to worry about. It's some hearts and doilies. Nothing lethal."

"You said that about the apple bob, that animatronic Santa Claus that went haywire and assaulted the townspeople whenever they came through the door, and what else was it...? Right, the Father Time figure who was anatomically correct underneath his robes."

I'd forgotten about that.

"He wasn't deadly."

"He was naked."

"I had no idea that the company I bought it from sold dirty novelties and not party decor. The website was very unclear."

"I just thank god it was an adult party and there were no children there."

Me, too. Wholeheartedly.

"I thought it was funny," Daisy declared, handing Jack his change. "People need to loosen up a bit. Everyone is so tense and uptight."

And Sheriff Jack Garrett was their spirit animal. Uptight didn't even begin to describe him. He was wound so tight he was a walking eight-day clock.

I stuck my tongue out at Jack. I never said I was mature. "Thank you, Daisy."

"You're welcome." Her gaze went to the door of the restaurant and her expression darkened. "Just what is he doing here? I told him he wasn't welcome. Sheriff, do your duty and arrest this man. He's trespassing."

This man was Colin Aiken, Daisy's ex-boyfriend. I didn't know much about him other than he didn't live in Ravenmist and he reminded me of a used car salesman. He was a little too smooth and way too in love with himself. For an older dude, he wasn't bad-looking. He'd kept himself trim and fit, and his hair was tinged with gray at the temples. He had a tan all year round despite the snow outside and always dressed in expensive clothes.

"I can't arrest him for just walking in, Daisy. He has to actually do something, like steal the cash register."

"He stole my trust, isn't that enough?"

Apparently not, because Jack allowed Colin to sidle up to Daisy, an icky smile on his face.

"Hey, baby. Miss me?"

His smarmy tone made me want to puke up my lunch.

"What are you doing here?" Daisy demanded, her hands wringing the kitchen towel until her knuckles were white. "I told you I never wanted to see you again."

"I knew you didn't mean it."

"I meant it."

"No, you don't. You're just angry and I don't blame you. But I'm back to make it all okay."

"Drop dead."

"You don't mean that, princess."

"Yes, I do."

"No, you don't."

Daisy put her hands on her hips, her face turning red. "Yes, I do. You cheated on me. No second chances."

"I'm not giving up. I'll be at the ball tonight."

"Thanks for the warning. Stay away from me."

Clearing his throat loudly, Jack stood and stepped between the two exes. "Time to go. I'll see you ladies at the party tonight. Colin? How about you and I have a little chat? Outside."

"I don't–"

Jack was having none of Colin's excuses. He hustled the other man out of the restaurant within seconds, leaving me and Daisy standing there in open-mouthed admiration. He hadn't taken no for an answer.

I had a million things to do for the party tonight, so I shrugged into my coat. "Jack's efficient. I'll give him that."

"You could do worse."

This entire town was love-crazy this week. I blamed the lace doily hearts.

"I'm not looking for a man."

"That's when it happens. That's how I found my Gavin." Daisy gave me a wink. "I think the sheriff is sweet on you."

I certainly hoped not. But just in case, I'd be sure to avoid him tonight.

Chapter Two

"YOU DON'T HAVE to go to the ball," I explained patiently to Terrence a few hours later. I'd retreated into my personal residence at the inn after a busy afternoon of preparations for the evening. I'd found Terrence kicking back in my living room watching a *Thin Man* movie. Ever since I'd subscribed to that movie channel for him, he'd shown himself much more often.

"Are the others going to the ball?"

When Terrence said *others,* he meant the spirits in town that hadn't crossed over. Like him.

"Maybe, I'm not sure. I know that Edward is."

Missy had told me yesterday that Edward, the ghost that haunted her bookstore, was coming to the ball tonight which puzzled me a little bit. It wasn't that anyone would notice there was a spirit at the party. Even if my guests weren't half in the bag from the booze, the paranormal energy in Ravenmist had reached such unprecedented levels that ghosts weren't in the least transparent. They were pale, but they appeared three dimensional. It was only if you reached out to touch them that you'd realize something wasn't quite right.

No, it wasn't that. It was…their clothing. It was my understanding that they wore what they'd died in and so far, I hadn't seen anyone that had bought the farm in a tux. Missy had been in a hurry and I hadn't had a chance to ask her about that. If Edward wasn't wearing a tuxedo he was going to stick out like a sore thumb and then somebody might notice that he wasn't quite alive.

Terrence sniffed disdainfully. "I don't like Edward. He thinks he's a bag of chips."

Did I mention that Terrence was watching other shows on television besides old movies? It was beginning to show in his vocabulary.

"I think the saying is *all that and a bag of chips*. And that's from the nineties. I don't think anyone says that anymore, but I could be wrong."

I hadn't said it originally, so I really didn't know.

Terrence, however, had a point. Edward certainly had his share of self-esteem and then some.

"Edward is from a different era than you are. That might explain it." I pulled my dress from the closet and hung it on the closet door. Black velvet with a halter bodice. I loved it. "What do you think of my dress?"

Terence dragged his gaze from the flat screen, inspecting the gown from the top to the hem. "I like it. It's more *Breakfast at Tiffany's* than Morticia Adams."

He might be watching too much television.

"That's what I was going for."

"Good job."

I dragged my black high-heeled pumps out of the back of the closet and placed them next to the dress. At some point this evening, when Missy and I were getting ready I was going to shoo Terrence out of the room. But in the meantime, he could darn well turn off the television and talk to me. I wanted to ask him a question that had been niggling at me since lunch.

"Terrence, have you heard the story of the Young Lovers?"

"Everyone has."

He was watching the television again.

I cleared my throat loudly. "Can you pause that movie?"

Terrence paused the film but sighed loudly. Excuse the heck out of me.

"So you know the story?"

"Everyone has, Tedi. It's famous."

"I was just thinking…you know…that you're about the right age…"

He wasn't picking up on my hint.

"What I'm trying to ask is if you know if the story is true. Did you know the Young Lovers?"

"No, but my mother told me the story. She might have. Why?"

"I just wondered if the story was true. Daisy was talking about it at lunch today and of course, Jack didn't believe it."

"Do you believe it?"

Did I? That was an interesting question, one I'd given far too much thought.

"I think like most legends the story has some basis in fact, but it's probably been twisted in some way to make it more exciting. I don't think that throwing a flower in the lake is going to make me happy in love."

"It doesn't matter if the story is true or not."

"Why not?"

"Because the story lives long after whatever happened. It's been given life."

What a nice way to describe it. So true, too.

Love might not last forever, but this legend just might.

THE VALENTINE BALL was in full swing and I'd survived another afternoon with Jack while he grilled me regarding the party decorations. Luckily, there were no sledgehammers or apple bobs. Mostly I'd decorated the inn with red and pink hearts, gleaming candelabras, and the piece de resistance – a life-sized figurine of Cupid complete with a golden bow and arrow.

Not anatomically correct. I checked. Cupid was currently presiding over the guests on the back deck.

The only two things Jack wasn't fond of were the candles and a champagne fountain located next to the buffet. Apparently, he didn't like open flames near fabric or alcohol that flowed freely. I explained that the dozens and dozens of candles were to set a romantic mood and the champagne was in case the candles didn't work. He'd backed off.

I'd then reminded him that this ball was a formal, black tie event and that I expected most guests to act with a bit of decorum. Ladies wouldn't want to ruin their dresses and the men had to return their rented tuxes the next day. They didn't want to lose their deposits.

I had to admit that the Valentine Ball was my second favorite event in Ravenmist – the Fall Festival being the first. I loved getting dressed up one night of the year and sipping champagne. I was wearing a floor-length black velvet gown and Missy had gone all out for the holiday theme, wearing a red lace dress that was the exact shade of her boyfriend Dylan's pocket square. She looked utterly amazing with the crimson gown and her long, dark hair.

"I think the sheriff is quite handsome. You could do a lot worse."

My best friend Missy was happily in love and that meant she wanted everyone else to be on Valentine's Day. She'd known me almost forever and she also knew why I wasn't the most enthusiastic person when it came to romance, so I was surprised that she wasn't letting the subject drop.

"Maybe I could do better."

"I'm sure you could."

She made it sound like she wasn't sure at all. Ouch. Did the whole town feel this way?

"We're friends and even that hasn't been easy. We're both extremely independent people who are most definitely not looking for love. We're not even strolling in that neighborhood."

"Sometimes you can end up where you least expect it."

That sounded like a poor way to walk through life. Aimlessly.

"That's true, but he's even more cynical than I am. I told him the Young Lovers story and he thinks it's a bunch of hooey." A thought occurred to me. "Is it? Your family would know."

Last October I'd learned that my very best friend in the world was a Reaper. She helped her uncle, the actual Grim Reaper, collect souls and send them on their journey to eternity. She had the black robes and everything. It was actually pretty cool.

Missy frowned. "Honestly, I don't know. I could check with my grandmother. She would probably know. We have to keep a record of the souls we escort and the ones that get away."

"That's...creepy."

"It's business. Speaking of creepy, has the sheriff mentioned seeing Terrence that night in your office?"

"Nope. It's like the whole incident never happened."

"That's weird. Do you think he's in denial?"

"I dunno, maybe. Terrence is thrilled, though, because he doesn't like people seeing him."

"Unlike Edward," Missy sighed. "He's here tonight along with a bunch of other ghosts. They have so much energy these days they can walk around the living without anyone even noticing they're a ghost. It's so strange."

I still hadn't figured out why all the spirits in Ravenmist had all of this energy and could appear completely opaque, just like a live human being. Missy had asked her family, but they hadn't had any ideas and had suggested a few books. That was Missy's territory and she was poring over them but had yet to find any helpful information. So for now, spirits walked freely in Ravenmist, hobnobbing with tourists and townspeople alike. Luckily, most of them had the good sense to keep to themselves.

And then there was Edward.

"I meant to ask you a question. I thought that they had to wear what they'd died in."

Missy's eyes went wide, which immediately put me on high alert. "Okay, now that's the really strange part of this."

Ghosts attending a party wasn't the weird part. Welcome to Ravenmist.

"What part?"

"Edward found an old tuxedo in someone's closet and he…put it on."

I was trying to picture it, but I couldn't get an image.

"I don't understand."

"Neither do I. It's as if he's full of so much energy that he almost has a body. He's real enough to wear clothes. He has to wear them over the clothes he already has on, but he can do it. Isn't that crazy?"

It was crazy, and I had yet to wrap my mind around it even when I caught sight of Edward mingling in the crowd. He looked happy and smiling, holding a glass of champagne which was entirely for show. Ghosts didn't eat or drink.

Or at least they didn't last time I checked. Bizarre things were happening here in town, so I couldn't completely discount it.

"Are they coming back to life?"

I hadn't put a voice to that question until now, but it had been in the far recesses of my mind.

Missy shook her head. "No way. This is just weird. But I have to say if this continues and they can hang out with the living then I can't see why many people would cross over. They'd just stay here and keep living their life. Going to work, hanging out with their friends. This is terrible for business. We need to figure out what's happening here and stop it."

"You have a point. Any progress on the reading?"

"None." Missy's serious expression turned to one of pure happiness. "There's Dylan. We're going to dance. You should ask the sheriff to dance."

"He's not even here."

"Yes, he is." Missy pointed to the front entrance. "He just walked in and looking very fine, if I do say so myself."

Jack did look good. He knew how to wear a tux but then he wore a uniform most days, so it wasn't a shock.

What was a surprise, however, were the four people standing behind Jack. My mom and dad, looking amazing all dressed up. But they weren't standing with each other.

They had dates.

I needed two aspirin and a Caribbean vacation.

Chapter Three

I DRAGGED MY mother away from her date but still close enough to see my dad talking to Jack. What on earth could they be talking about? And who was that woman on my dad's arm? She didn't look at all familiar.

"Mom, what are you doing?"

My mother, Peggy Hamilton, knew exactly why I was freaking out, but she acted like she didn't have a clue, her expression humorously blank.

"What do you mean, dear?"

"I mean, who is that man that you're with?"

"You know him, Theodosia. He's the new principal at the high school. Everett Wagner."

I'd vaguely seen him around town but never spoken to him. He looked different all dressed up.

"Are you on a date?" I hissed. "You're not divorced yet."

Peggy's chin went up. "Your father and I are legally separated. Besides, he's here with a date, too. Aren't you upset with him?"

"I'll get to him in a minute. Who is she, anyway?"

"I have no idea." Mom leaned in close so she could whisper in my ear. "But between you and me I don't think she thought through that dress. The sapphire color is terrible against her pale skin."

A catty remark. A good sign that my mom was a little jealous. Dad used to go all out on Valentine's Day with a fancy dinner, flowers, candy, and usually a gift, too. Mom had to be missing that.

"Goodness, doesn't Daisy look gorgeous?"

Daisy and her new boyfriend Gavin had just walked into the inn wearing two of the biggest smiles I'd seen all evening. They really did look in love, and although I hoped it wasn't contagious, I was truly happy for them.

Peggy patted my arm. "She does look lovely. See? You're never too old to fall in love. I'm going to get some champagne, dear. I'll talk to you later. You should go ask the sheriff to dance."

Was that the only thing anyone could say tonight? My mother was off before I had to reply, and Daisy was there giving me a big hug. For tonight she'd tossed away her tie-dyed t-shirts but not the bright colors. Her dress was a rainbow of gossamer that swirled around her ankles and she was wearing her hand-crafted jewelry. Gavin was in the usual black tuxedo. They looked like the perfect couple.

"You two are like the prom king and queen," I teased. "The rest of us are just lowly peasants."

Daisy blushed from the compliment. "You're too sweet, and

you're hardly a peasant. You look beautiful tonight. So classy. You should ask the sheriff to dance."

I heaved a heavy inward sigh.

"That does seem to be the prevailing wisdom tonight, but I am the hostess which means I have responsibilities. In fact, I need to go check on the kitchen. There's a lot of hungry people here tonight and I don't want a riot on my hands."

After another hug, I made a beeline for the kitchen where my capable chef had it all under control. He'd had a "moment" earlier today when I'd asked him about the mini quiches but since then it had been smooth sailing. I didn't really need to check on him, but the party was beginning to get to me. First Edward wearing clothes, then my parents on dates with other people, and finally everyone and their brother telling me to dance with Jack.

I was three feet from the kitchen and almost home free when my dad and his date stepped into my path, his arm around her waist. It appeared that I was going to have to deal with this right now whether I liked it or not.

"Pumpkin, I wanted you to meet Kate. Kate Beckswith."

The name didn't ring any bells for me. She had to be new in town or perhaps she didn't live in Ravenmist at all.

"It's very nice to meet you, Kate. I hope you're enjoying the ball. Is this your first Valentine's Ball?"

The woman smiled and glanced at my dad briefly before answering. "Actually, it is. I lived in Ravenmist in my youth, but I moved away before I was old enough to attend."

An attractive woman with sparkling blue eyes and dark hair, Kate showed off a trim figure in her sapphire blue gown. She appeared to be slightly younger than my dad, but some women had all the luck and simply didn't age much. Perhaps they had gone to school together?

"Are you back for good or just visiting?"

"I'm back for good." She and my dad sort of stared into each other's eyes for a long moment, possibly forgetting that I or the other people in the room even existed. It seemed like everyone wanted to get into the romance tonight. "I've missed this little town. I'm happy to be home."

It occurred to me that this wasn't their first date. Or probably even their second.

"We're happy to have you home," my father said. "This little town gets in your blood, doesn't it? Tedi left for the big city but she came back as well."

Kate clasped her hands together in delight. "I guess we have something in common. I'd love to hear what brought you back sometime."

My story wasn't all that interesting...or appropriate for a night like tonight. An evening for lovers.

"We should all get together for coffee or lunch," my dad suggested. "Once the craziness dies down from tonight's party you should have a lull in your schedule."

I certainly would, and I planned to enjoy every single second of being almost bored.

"We can talk the beginning of the week," I replied when I

realized they were waiting for me to say something. "Shoot me a text."

The band began playing "Isn't It Romantic" and Kate's face lit up. "I love this song."

"Then we must dance to it," Dad said with a grin. "Please excuse us, Tedi."

My father whirled Kate onto the dance floor with a flourish, joining the throng of people in the main room of the inn. Almost every piece of furniture had been moved to one of the outbuildings on the property to make room for the band and the partiers. It was a pain, but it was worth it.

"I thought you'd be dancing."

Whirling around, I came face to face with Jack who did, indeed, look good in a tuxedo up close as well. Luckily, I was older and wiser now and I wasn't going to fall for a pretty face. I wasn't going to fall at all, as a matter of fact.

"I'm the hostess. We don't get to have fun."

"Is that a rule?"

"More of a guideline, but I've found it to be true more often than not."

Glancing out to the sea of dancers, Jack nodded. "Then how about you and me take a turn on the dance floor? One quick one."

My eyes narrowed suspiciously. What was he up to? If he'd suddenly gone sweet on me, I wasn't sure we could be still be friends.

"Why?"

"Why?" he echoed. "Why not?"

"I could think of a myriad of reasons."

Sighing, he rolled his eyes and immediately reminded me of his son Tyler. "Fine. People are driving me crazy about asking you to dance so I thought if we got it over with, they might leave me alone. Happy now?"

Very happy.

"Now that's a reason I can respect. One quick dance and then we avoid each other all night. It's a plan. You know, you have to learn to tune out the town busybodies. I have."

"They've been bugging you, too?"

"As if you were the last man on earth." I looked around the room and then raised my eyebrows at Jack. "Clearly you are not."

"Thanks for that. I think. Shall we?"

We shall, we would, and then hopefully everyone would leave us the heck alone.

JACK TURNED OUT to be a decent dancer despite his bad leg where he'd been shot on duty in Chicago. He kept it simple and we did fine, although our one little dance attracted quite a bit of attention. Even my parents were wearing knowing smiles on their faces as if they'd set the whole thing up themselves.

Once the song ended though, we immediately separated. I headed toward the kitchen and Jack went…somewhere else. I didn't actually know where he was going, and I didn't think to ask. We'd done our civic duty and frankly, sparks hadn't flown. I hadn't fallen head over heels for him and he hadn't for me either from the look of things. We'd had a pleasant dance and I hadn't hated it. For Jack and me, that was progress. Not that long ago we'd barely been able to be in the same room. Now we were boogieing to the oldies.

I was checking the supply of canapés on the buffet when I heard a ruckus in the back of the ballroom. Loud voices. Louder than the music and that was saying something because the band was on fire tonight. Hurrying to that section of the inn, I found Daisy, Gavin, Colin, and another woman arguing and none of them looking pleased. Gavin's hands were furled into fists and I probably had about thirty seconds to intervene before he threw a punch.

Slipping my own body between the men, I tried to make myself physically larger than I really was to push them apart. I'd seen Jack do it one night at the local watering hole and I'd admired his technique at diffusing a tense situation.

"Easy there," I said in a firm tone. "This is a party. Let's keep it civil."

Daisy pointed to her former lover. "I don't want him here."

The yet-to-be-identified woman pointed to Daisy. "Well, I don't want you here either."

"What is going on here?" I said in my most authoritative tone. "I don't want any trouble at this party tonight."

"I came over to talk to Daisy," Colin said, his cheeks a ruddy shade. "That's all."

The woman wasn't happy about that, apparently. "You're not supposed to be talking to other women."

Daisy laughed out loud. "Good luck with that. He's a womanizer, honey. Get used to it."

"I am not," Colin protested. "I never cheated on you."

"Tell it to someone who cares," Daisy replied. "I have someone better now."

Gavin nodded, his face still bright red but his hands had relaxed slightly. "Daisy doesn't need you anymore so hit the road. You're not wanted here."

"If he cheated on me, he'll cheat on you," Daisy warned the other woman. "Don't be stupid."

"Don't call me stupid." The woman glared at Daisy. "I think you're trying to steal him."

I couldn't think of one reason anyone would try and steal Colin but maybe she knew something about him that I didn't.

Daisy began to protest but I shook my head and placed my hand on her shoulder to guide her away from this altercation. It looked like Colin needed to deal with his girlfriend and leave Daisy out of it all.

"Why don't you and Gavin try the buffet? I think the chef was going to put out some mini cheesecakes."

The couple wasn't fooled by my offer. They were well aware I was trying to keep the peace. That goal became exponentially easier when Jack appeared out of nowhere, pushing himself between the two men and practically lifting me up and placing me out of harm's way.

Hey, I wasn't doing that badly. But I welcomed his interference. This was his specialty, after all.

"There have been some complaints about the noise," Jack said in that cop voice that he used so frequently. "What seems to be the problem?"

The woman pointed to Daisy, her lips pressed together in a thin line. Normally she was probably quite an attractive woman with her dark hair and big brown eyes, but tonight she was red with fury. My personal thought was that she was mad at the wrong person. She should be angry with Colin. "She's trying to steal my man."

Jack's brows shot up and he looked Colin from head to toe. "That's one interpretation. Now why don't we step some place more private and talk this through? Like adults."

Gavin raised his hands in surrender. "I don't want any trouble. We just want to enjoy the party without this guy bothering Daisy. She doesn't want anything to do with him."

Jack had witnessed the conversation between Colin and Daisy this morning, so he had a decent idea what was going on. He nodded to Gavin. "That's fine. I just need a word with Colin then. Let's step into the drawing room."

With a firm hand on Colin's elbow, Jack steered the man and the angry woman into my drawing room despite their protests that none of this was their fault. I shooed a few of the other guests out and from the expressions on their faces this was going to hit the gossip mill faster than the speed of light.

Life in a small town. Or at least, life in Ravenmist.

My dad and Kate must have heard the ruckus because they'd abandoned the dance floor and were standing outside the drawing room wearing matching concerned expressions. "Trouble, pumpkin?"

"Just a misunderstanding. Nothing that Jack can't handle."

Dad nodded. "He's a good one. Still…we could hear the arguing all the way over near the dining room."

That meant pretty much everyone heard it. Lovely.

"Daisy's ex was bugging her a little but Jack is talking to him. It's all under control."

"We heard two women's voices," Kate said. "Was there someone else?"

The whole story was going to be talked about tomorrow anyway.

"Yes, his girlfriend is also here. Let's just say there is more than one misunderstanding tonight."

"Some men shouldn't be allowed around females," Kate sighed. "Cheaters and liars. They never learn."

"I don't know the details."

And I hope that I never do. I adored Daisy, but I didn't want to hear the particulars of her love life.

Dad placed his arm around Kate's shoulders. "Since everything is okay, we'll get back to the party. I think I need something cool to drink."

With a wave, they were headed to the bar area and I was left to enter my drawing room where there were several voices. Loud.

And all talking at once. I wanted to place my hands over my ears.

Jack held up his hands, his voice authoritative. "Now let's quiet down. I'm going to talk for a minute."

Colin and the female fell silent but didn't look all that happy about it. I doubted that Jack cared, though.

"Now," he began, his arms crossed over his chest. "I'm going to say a few things and you're going to listen. Do I make myself clear?"

At first, I didn't think they were going to agree but when Jack didn't budge, they reluctantly nodded their heads.

"Good. I'll start with Colin." Jack turned his attention to the squirming man in the disheveled tuxedo. "Daisy doesn't want anything to do with you and you are going to respect that. I want you to stay away from her. If you don't, you and I are going to have a problem. Do I make myself clear?"

Colin opened his mouth to protest but something in Jack's eyes must have stopped him because the words died on his lips. "I just wanted to talk to her."

The woman fumed next to Colin, looking like she was ready to sock him in the eye. This was why I avoided love and relationships.

"She doesn't want to talk to you," Jack replied evenly. "She wants you to leave her alone and that's what I want you to do as well. Any issues with that?"

"No," Colin said, his head hung down. "I can do that."

"Good," stated Jack, then turning his attention to the female.

"Now I don't think we've been introduced. I'm Jack Garrett, the sheriff in town. And you are?"

The woman shot a death glare at Colin before answering. "Jane. Jane Allerton. I'm Colin's girlfriend. Or at least I thought I was."

Another dark glare.

I kind of felt sorry for Jane. She'd thought she was the only one and now she could easily see that Colin was a dog that wasn't going to give up chasing cars. She might try and frame the situation as Daisy's fault, but she'd have to be lying to herself to believe it.

"Can I give you some advice?"

"Okay…"

Jane didn't sound too sure, but she let the sheriff continue.

"Some men just don't want to settle down. Find one that does. Your life will be easier and a heck of a lot more peaceful."

I could have had that embroidered on a pillow at one point during my divorce. Wise words. To my surprise, Jane seemed to take them to heart. She pulled out her phone and began to dial.

"I'm going to call a cab." She elbowed Colin who had been uncharacteristically quiet the last few minutes before turning on her heel and marching toward the door. "For myself."

"Should I do the same for you?" Jack asked. "Have you been drinking?"

Colin lifted his head and tried to stand tall after watching his girlfriend dump him in front of virtual strangers. "I have not. I don't drink at all. I'm good to drive."

"Then I suggest you go home. Alone."

Without another word Colin exited the drawing room, leaving myself and Jack alone. It would be lovely if I could get through just one party without having to deal with unruly guests.

"Do you think he'll take your advice?" I asked Jack as I fell back into the overstuffed sofa with a sigh. "I don't know him well, but he doesn't seem like he's a great listener."

"If he's smart, he will," Jack growled, lowering himself into a Queen Anne chair that had been my Grandmother Rose's favorite.

Jack and I had a little "thing" going the past few months. It had all started with an innocent bet about the neighborhood kids toilet-papering his house. I'd won twenty bucks off of him and he'd been trying to get it back since.

"I think you answered my question," I said, waggling my eyebrows. "I've got a twenty in my purse – your twenty – that he won't take your advice."

That twenty had been passed back and forth for the last three and a half months.

Tapping his chin, Jack grinned. "I would like that money back. Let me see…did I scare him enough? I think I did. I'll take that bet."

"Sucker."

"We'll see, won't we?"

With any luck I wouldn't see Colin's face at this ball for the rest of the night.

MY FEET WERE killing me, and I desperately wanted to kick off these high heels and replace them with a pair of warm, comfy slippers. If I couldn't get the final guests out of the inn in the next thirty minutes, I was going to do it anyway. As usual there were a few people who didn't want the party to end and I was going to have to be the bad guy and send them home.

The kitchen door swung open and Jack strode in, barely glancing at the stacks of dirty dishes all around him. Earlier those stacks had been trays of food destined for the buffet and we'd both eaten far more than we should have.

"I cannot believe people are still here," he declared over the din of the staff cleaning up. Kitchens were always loud and busy, at least in my experience. "Don't they have homes?"

"Theoretically. I didn't realize you were still here. I thought you left hours ago."

"I was planning to and then I thought you might want help at the end of the evening getting rid of people. I can see that I was right."

There was nothing Jack loved more than being right. Glad I could give him that gift tonight.

"How are you planning to help me? Shoot into the air and watch them scatter?"

He gave me a look that said he didn't appreciate my sass at this point in the evening. So noted.

"I was going to tell them that they had to leave and then call them a cab."

"You're a cab."

He regarded me quizzically, his head tilted to the side. "What?"

"You're a cab. Get it? You were going to call them a cab…"

Seriously? This man had no sense of humor whatsoever. This was a classic joke and I was hilarious.

"Don't quit your day job."

Sniffing disdainfully, I beckoned to him. "Let's go send everyone home. My feet are killing me."

"I don't know how you women walk around in those heels."

"Societal expectations."

There were a few loiterers in the dining room and bar, but they were easy to dislodge and happy to return to their own hearth and home. There were still partiers in the main room, however, and from the sound of their laughter they might be a tougher nut to crack.

I'd underestimated the sheriff's mad skills at ejecting people, however. He gently but firmly pried the guests from the dance floor and moved them expeditiously toward the exit. He didn't use any brute force, only his charm, which I hated to admit that he possessed.

With barely a glance in my direction, Jack headed out of the back doors. "Are there any stranglers outside?"

"I doubt it. It's too cold."

With my sore feet, I struggled to keep up with his long legs. The cold air quickly seeped through the thin material of my dress, raising goosebumps on my flesh. Jack's tuxedo jacket was made of wool, so I doubted he even noticed the temperature.

Just as he'd predicted, there was one person left who had apparently had a little too much to drink and passed out, sitting in the gazebo. Dear God, how long had he been out here? He might have hypothermia. How much alcohol did a person need in their blood to protect them from freezing to death?

"Should I call an ambulance, Jack? We don't know how long he's been passed out here."

"Yes, give them a call just in case. I'll see if I can wake him up."

Thankfully my cell phone was practically an extra appendage and I immediately began dialing.

"Hey, buddy. Time to wake up," Jack said, his voice louder to hopefully wake our sleeping guest. "I've called you a taxi and you can sleep at home."

The man didn't move, and I was beginning to get a funny feeling in the pit of my stomach. A familiar sensation like right before I took a math test. Now that I was taking a much closer look at the last party guest, I was thinking that from the back he looked kind of familiar. Of course, all the men were in tuxedos so to some extent they looked alike but that haircut… I knew it but couldn't quite place it whether due to fatigue, too much champagne, or something entirely different.

"Time to wake up," Jack said even louder this time, placing his hand on the man's shoulder lightly. The figure lurched forward and then to the side, exposing his face for the first time.

I gasped at the sight before me, my knees immediately going weak.

Colin. With an arrow right through his heart.

"You can tell the ambulance they don't need to hurry. He's dead."

And there were at least two women who had motive to want him that way.

Chapter Four

"**I**F YOU COULD stop throwing parties where people end up dead that would be great," Jack growled as he and I hovered a few feet from Colin Aiken's body. The coroner was now attending to him and getting ready to pronounce him dead, and until then Jack wasn't allowed to do much.

"Two," I replied between gritted teeth, holding up two fingers. "Two parties. It's not like it's an epidemic or anything. Just two."

Although it was two more than I would have preferred.

"At least your Santa statue only smacked around a few guests," Jack continued as if I hadn't spoken. "That wasn't too bad, and we just turned him off. Now we have another dead man, Tedi."

As if I didn't know that.

"I didn't kill him. This isn't my fault." A good defense was a better offense. "Maybe this is all your fault. We didn't have any murder in Ravenmist until you became sheriff."

Jack didn't get to return my fire because the coroner, old Doc Harris, had concluded his brief examination.

"Well…he's dead."

Old Doc Harris was about a hundred and thirty years old and he'd lost most of his hearing, so his pronouncement was made at the top of his lungs, almost like the sound of a cannon. People could hear him for miles.

Bless Jack, he didn't growl or show any frustration, instead calmly nodding as though the doctor hadn't just made the most obvious of declarations.

"Any idea of the time of death or mode?"

"I'm guessing it was that arrow through his heart. You'll know more after the postmortem."

Which he wouldn't perform. He had a younger colleague that did those for him in the basement of the local hospital.

Doc Harris glanced at the deceased as he shrugged into his winter coat. "As for time of death, he's not even in rigor yet so less than four hours. My estimate based on liver temperature is two."

That would put poor Colin's death at around midnight. Straining my brain, I tried to think of what I was doing at that time. Kitchen? Yes, that's probably where I was although I wasn't sure it mattered. With so many people milling in every corner of the inn, I doubted I'd notice if someone slipped off with Cupid's bow and arrow.

I felt a hand on my shoulder and then I heard my best friend Missy's voice. "Um, Tedi. I need to talk to you."

Really? Now?

"This isn't the best time. Can it wait?"

"No."

Frowning, I took a good look at her, noticing that she wore a peculiar expression that I'd never seen before. Which was saying something because I'd known her since I was five. You'd think in almost thirty years I would have seen just about every expression she had, but this one was new.

"Will you excuse me, Jack?"

Of course, the sheriff was barely paying any attention to me, his focus all on poor Colin, so I was able to slip away with Missy to a quiet corner of the room.

"What's going on? What can't wait?"

She rolled her eyes and sighed. "We have a runner."

I didn't follow.

"A runner?" I echoed. "I don't understand."

Missy leaned forward, her glance darting over to the sheriff and his two deputies and then back to me. "Colin Aiken. He's made a run for it. He didn't want to cross over, and he ran off. I don't know where he is. He was really freaked out, Tedi. I'm actually worried about him."

"Can he...hurt himself?"

I felt stupid asking the question, but I wasn't completely up on all of this grim reaper/dead people stuff.

"He's dead. So...no."

"Don't look at me like that. I don't know about these things."

"I'm just worried about him. He was acting crazed, pacing around and in major denial. When I talked to him about moving toward the light he panicked and ran."

It was a question I had been thinking about since I'd seen Colin's body. The arrow was right in the center of his chest...

"Do you think he might have seen his killer? Did he say anything about that? That might explain why he was so upset."

Missy shook her head. "He didn't say anything about that but that doesn't mean he didn't see them. It's not uncommon for people to be upset and angry but they normally don't run from me. That has me concerned."

"Where can he go? Do ghosts have boundaries? Like he can't leave town?"

"I've never heard of any. I think he can go wherever he wants, although he might not have enough energy to get far. He's so new."

I'd remembered Missy's bookstore ghost Edward saying that he gained more and more energy as time went on, but the surge of power that Ravenmist was experiencing made anything possible.

"Do you have to go after him?"

Missy shrugged. "I don't have to, technically. He refused my services and that's enough, but I am worried about him. I'd like to speak with him again and calm him down. I hate to think of him out there scared and all by himself."

Colin may not have been my favorite person, but I didn't like that idea, either.

"I'll help you. Jack doesn't want me around right now anyway. Where do we start?"

"I thought we could check the grounds. Maybe he didn't get far."

"I'll get my coat."

This put a whole new spin on ghost hunting.

NOTE TO SELF. It's freakin' cold in the middle of the night in February. Think about that next time before agreeing to tromp out in the snow looking for a runaway ghost. My clothes and wool coat weren't much protection from the weather.

I couldn't feel my lips or ears.

Surely, they were going to fall off any minute, dropping onto the frozen ground like a snowman gone very wrong. The temperature was positively inhuman and the wind sweeping across the flat land was whipping my wool scarf all over the place and occasionally smacking me in the eye.

The only light was from the crescent moon, so we had to watch every step lest we trip over a tree stump or our own feet. This wasn't the smartest thing I'd ever done. In fact, it was downright stupid. I'd slipped out the back door before Jack could see me go because I hadn't wanted him to question me. He would have a fit if he knew I was out here in the middle of the night.

"When we both die out here of exposure who will escort our souls to the light?"

Missy frowned and pursed her lips. "I guess my mom could

fill in temporarily until my cousin could take over."

"Aren't you cold?" I asked in an accusing tone. While I was hunched over in an attempt to avoid the wind, Missy didn't appear to be bothered in the least. "Is it because you're a supernatural being?"

"No, it's because I'm wearing long underwear under my clothes."

We'd both changed out of our gowns before going out, but I'd been in such a hurry I hadn't even thought about long underwear. Darn it.

"I'm freezing, and we haven't seen hide nor hair of Colin. Maybe he's left town."

"I really don't see how he would have the energy to do that. He has to be close by."

"He was over by the pond a little while ago."

A voice in the air above my ear. A few months ago, I might have been freaked out but now I was much calmer. That voice belonged to Edward.

A ghost.

Missy stopped in her tracks, her gloved hands on her hips. "Show yourself, Edward. This isn't one of your games."

Edward lived in Missy's bookstore and he did like to play little jokes now and then, like rearranging shelves and hiding the coffee. Missy – and I – took coffee very seriously.

He appeared right in front us slowly, his figure becoming more and more solid with every passing second. Within a minute, he looked like a living, breathing human and not the specter that he actually was. At some point he must have shed his tuxedo because he was back in his regular clothes – dark pants and white button-down shirt. No coat, of course. Ghosts don't get hypothermia. As always, I was struck by how young he looked. He could have been any young man in the mid-twentieth century.

"You've seen Colin?" Missy demanded. "We need to find him. He's very upset."

Edward leaned his shoulder against a bare oak tree, the branches covered in snow. "I saw your runaway about fifteen minutes ago. He was heading toward the forest."

There was a small forest at the back of my property past the clearing, the pond, and an old barn that we used for storage. It belonged to the county and they were always threatening to tear all of the trees down and widen the main road into town. If Colin was there, we'd never find him, at least in the dark.

"Did you talk to him?" Missy asked. "Did he say anything?"

"No," Edward replied. His figure growing dimmer and then much brighter. He had probably used up a great deal of energy tonight to mingle among the living. "Why would I talk to him? I don't know him."

"Because he was upset?" Missy said between clenched teeth. "You must know how he feels."

"He's upset that he's dead," Edward said bluntly. "It's not an exclusive club. He'll get used to it. In the meantime, he'll be fine. He's already dead. He can't get any deader."

Edward had a point. He was also slowly fading away.

"You're disappearing," I said, pointing out the obvious. "Are you okay?"

"Just tired. I'm going to back to the bookstore and get some rest."

With those words he was gone as quickly as he'd appeared.

"He was absolutely no help," Missy said with a groan. "At this rate, we'll never find Colin Aiken."

"Has Edward ever been much help? At all?"

"No," she admitted. "But I live in hope. Maybe we could call to Colin? He might answer."

He might. Or anyone who overheard us might think we had a screw loose calling to a dead man.

"We can give it a try."

"Where have you been?"

The first words out of Jack's mouth when I returned to the inn, almost frozen to death. I'd snuck in my private entrance only to find Terrence watching old movies on the television. Quickly, I'd shed my winter gear and splashed warm water on my face to get rid of my ruddy cheeks, hoping no one would notice.

"I got out of the way. Isn't that what you wanted me to do?"

Giving me a strange look, he shrugged. "Yes, but you never do it, so I was shocked."

"I'll overlook that remark. Have you made any progress?"

"If you're asking if I know who did it, the answer is no. How many times do I have to tell you that these investigations take time?"

"One hundred and six."

"If I'd stayed in Chicago, I wouldn't have to put up with this."

"If you'd stayed in Chicago, I wouldn't be offering to fix you something to eat in my state-of-the-art kitchen."

His eyes lit up and he actually looked hopeful. "Seriously? Because I'm starving."

"The chef's gone for the evening but I can whip up some scrambled eggs and toast. If you're not too picky."

"Cheese in the eggs?"

"Cheese in the eggs."

Jack followed me into the kitchen and perched on a stool while I fixed him a small breakfast. Enough for two because now that I'd hiked through the freezing cold for about an hour, I'd also worked up an appetite.

Placing a hot plate of food in front of him, I sat down next to him. "So what have you found out?"

"I knew breakfast would have a price."

"It's a pretty cheap price. What did you find out?" I popped a piece of toast into my mouth. "You know you want to tell me."

"I do? Okay, I'll tell you that Colin Aiken is not the most loved man in the world. I checked his cell phone and he had several angry texts tonight from what appears to be two other women."

"That doesn't surprise me. He had that vibe."

Jack's fork paused in midair a few inches from his mouth. "That vibe?"

"Women pick up on these things when we get a little older and more experienced with men. If you pay attention you can spot it a mile away and keep your distance."

"Women can have that vibe, too."

I'd never asked Jack about his past relationships and although we were friends now, I still didn't want to. It seemed far too personal. He hadn't asked me about my ex, either.

"They can," I agreed. "It's too bad that most of us learn it the hard way."

Jack shoveled the last of eggs into his mouth. "You're not a bad cook."

"It's scrambled eggs, not a soufflé. But thank you. Now what else did you find out?"

"Not much. I checked Aiken's car outside and I didn't see anything out of the ordinary. I have a buddy of mine in Chicago checking finances. He might have owed money to the wrong people. I also spoke to the few staff that hadn't already left the party. They don't remember anything out of the ordinary, either. As soon as the sun's up I'll need to speak to the guests at the party."

There was a whole bunch unsaid in Jack's statement.

"You mean you want to talk to Daisy."

Jack paused before answering. "Yes. Her boyfriend, too."

"Gavin," I replied automatically. "His name is Gavin Baldwin. He's a dairy farmer."

"I'll need to talk to Gavin and also to Jane. Plus, anyone else that might have harbored a grudge against Aiken. For all we know he has a passel of ex-wives and swindled business partners."

"Daisy didn't kill him."

Sighing, Jack wiped his mouth with the paper napkin. "I don't think that she did, Tedi, but I have to speak with her. You know how this works."

"Daisy is completely nonviolent. She's a pacifist."

"I'm sure that she is but I still need to question her. I wouldn't be doing my job if I didn't."

"Then you'll find out that she didn't do it."

"Don't do this. Don't get involved like last time. This is police business. Stick to running the inn."

I hadn't wanted to get involved the first time, but he had thought that Missy was a killer. She wasn't a killer any more than Daisy was.

"I'm not going to get involved. I just wanted to make sure that you knew that there was no way Daisy could have done something like this."

"I've got it. Now that you've said your piece will you stay out of my murder investigation?"

I waved away his concern as if it was nothing. "Of course. I have plenty of other work to do. I don't need to do your job, too."

Unless he tried to blame Daisy. Then I just might have to help him out a bit.

Chapter Five

A FEW HOURS later when the sun was up, Missy and I headed to her grandmother's place to ask her about the Young Lovers and whether there was any truth in the story. Ada Lawrence lived just outside of Ravenmist in an old farmhouse that looked like something out of a storybook. The old Victorian had been around for over a hundred years but had been lovingly maintained by the family. Most recently it had been painted a china blue with white trim. In the spring and summer there were flowers all around it but in the winter the expansive front lawn was carpeted in sparkling white snow.

We didn't even have to knock. The door flew open and Ada, gray-haired and dressed in her usual brightly-colored track suit, waved us in to the kitchen where she immediately sat us down and fed us apple pie and hot chocolate. My chef could make some awesome desserts, but Ada's apple pie had witchcraft in it. The cocoa was darn good too and warmed my insides nicely.

This was always the hardest part of winter. The holidays were over and there was not much to look forward to except spring. Business at the inn would be slow until then and I hoped to enjoy every moment of the respite.

I did everything but lick the plate clean. Ada offered me a second piece of pie, but I didn't want to waddle out to the car when we left. I'd already put on my usual five pounds of winter weight thanks to all the goodies around Thanksgiving and Christmas.

"Gran, we were wondering if you knew about the Young Lovers. Are they real?" Missy asked after the plates were cleared and the hot chocolate was refilled.

Ada frowned as she sipped her cocoa. "I have no idea. I was never curious enough to look, to be honest. I always assumed it was a story to bring in tourists."

Missy laughed. "You sound like the new sheriff. He's so cynical."

"He's a nice-looking man." Ada gave me a pointed look, her brows raised. "You could do worse, you know."

"That seems to be the prevailing wisdom. I'm not in the market for a man."

"That's when you find them," Ada chuckled, levering up from her chair. "Let me go get the book and see what it says."

Missy had already explained to me that her family kept detailed records on every dead soul they were assigned. If two young people drowned, there would be an entry in *the book*.

I'd had a picture of *the book* in my head. Some ancient leather-bound tome the size of an end table with gold engraving on the outside and that particularly musty smell. It didn't look like any of that at all.

Ada returned with her iPad.

She laughed when she saw my mouth hanging open. "We digitized all the records a few years ago. Makes it easier on these old bones than lugging around huge, dusty books and then paging through them one by one. With this new database all we have to do is a search on *drowning*."

Missy nodded in agreement. "Like everyone else we have to keep up with technology."

In a way I was comforted by the notion that the Grim Reaper wasn't using parchment and quill pens anymore.

Ada's fingers tapped on the screen. "There have been several drownings through the years according to this but you're looking for a male and female that would have died at the same time. Let's see…yes, here it is. Hmmm, long before my time. Charles Baker and Amelia Croft, both age sixteen. They died on July 10th of 1874 at ten-thirty. They were escorted to the light by…wait."

Ada tapped on the screen a few more times. "They didn't cross over."

I gasped in surprise and Missy's eyes had gone round.

"Does it say why?" I asked, leaning forward to try and see what Ada was looking at. "Why wouldn't they go into the light?"

The older woman shook her head. "It doesn't say. We didn't keep records of reasons back then. That didn't happen until the twentieth century. But the entry is very clear. They didn't cross over."

Missy finally found her voice. "Could they have crossed over later and it didn't get noted in the original entry?"

"All the books were digitized, so it would be in the database if they had, even if it was entered into a later hardbound book. No, they're still spirits, although they may have moved on from Ravenmist for all we know. They may not even be active." Ada smiled and stood again, turning to rummage in a kitchen drawer. "That reminds me. You asked about the increased spirit energy in town and if I knew anything about it. I don't but I do have the name of a medium that might be able to help you. She might be able to tell you what's going on. If I can find it…here it is."

Ada handed Missy a cream-colored business card with black writing.

Missy didn't look impressed. "Madame Harriet? For real?"

"For real is right," Ada replied firmly. "She's the real deal, not one of these grifters looking for a quick buck. She might be able to help you, although my personal opinion is that we're in a new cycle and this too will end at some point. It's the circle of life."

Or in this case, the circle of the dead.

"Thanks, Gran." Missy tucked the card into her handbag. "We'll give her a call. Now we really should be going. There's been a murder at the inn again."

"I heard about that. Did you get him into the light?"

Missy's smile fell. "No, he ran away. We tried to find him but he's hiding and upset."

"He'll come around. Most of them do eventually."

With a wave we said goodbye to Ada and climbed into the

vehicle. Missy didn't say much until the old Victorian was out of sight.

"I want to find those two Young Lovers, Tedi. Maybe they're ready to cross over."

No surprise. I knew she was going to want to do that.

"And you want me to help you."

"Do you have anything better to do?"

What were friends for if not to hunt spirits in the freezing cold? This time I wouldn't forget my long underwear.

MISSY DROPPED ME off at the inn and Jack's official SUV was still parked in front. In a loading zone. I don't know where my green grocer unloaded this week's fruit and vegetables, but I had a feeling I was going to get an earful about his bad back. He complained about it at the best of times.

I found Jack in the first place I looked for him which was the kitchen. He was chomping on a steak sandwich with a side of crinkle cut fries. I felt badly for his arteries but the aroma from the food smelled delicious. My apple pie suddenly seemed very long ago.

"I'm beginning to think that I should be charging you rent, Jack. Every time I turn around…there you are."

"Stop throwing parties with dead bodies and you'll see less of me."

I ignored the jibe and poured myself a cup of coffee from the carafe in the corner. It was always kept full throughout the day and although I shouldn't have another cup, I needed the caffeine. Missy and I were going to find the Young Lovers later tonight. I was already running on a sleep deficit.

"Seriously, I thought you'd be out running down clues and questioning suspects."

"It's hard to concentrate with an empty stomach."

"I'm glad I could help with that. You know, you can eat out in the dining room with the rest of the guests."

"I could, but then I'd be interrupted every five seconds by people asking me about the murder last night."

That made sense. He was hiding in my kitchen and I couldn't blame him. I'd done it a time or two myself.

"So…have you learned anything yet?"

He had to have known that if I found him in my noisy kitchen I was definitely going to ask.

Taking his time before answering, Jack chewed his sandwich thoughtfully and then nodded.

"A few things."

"Such as?"

"Why should I tell you?"

Ah, we were going to play this game again.

"Why not? It will be all over Ravenmist by dinnertime. At least you can have the peace of knowing that the correct details are out and not some wild story they made up at the beauty shop or the newsstand."

Jack simply grinned at my logic. "It's funny that you think

that peace of mind is important to me. But…I will tell you that the estimated time of death was indeed around midnight."

That meant that he was killed at the height of the party when the inn and even the grounds outside – thanks to portable heaters – was crowded with people.

"Anyone could have done it then."

"I'm not sure that I'm in agreement there, Tedi. The place was packed with bodies and yet someone was able to steal the bow and arrow without being seen, and then found the opportunity to shoot Aiken. That doesn't sound easy and I don't think just anyone could have pulled that off."

Okay, that did sound rather complex.

"I hadn't thought about the details, only the opportunity."

"In that you are correct – many people had opportunity but only a few had motive. That we know of, of course. There may be dozens, if not hundreds of people that hated Colin Aiken."

"And it's your job to find them all."

He held up his hands and shook his head. "Now wait a minute. I only need to find the killer. Hating Aiken isn't against the law. In fact, it might be a wise course of action."

Sliding onto a barstool next to Jack's, I attempted to act casual, crossing my legs and propping my chin on my hand. "So who do you think might have a motive? Jane?"

"Jane," Jack agreed with a nod. "Gavin Baldwin. And Daisy."

That was exactly what I was afraid of.

"Daisy would never do something like that. Get real. She's a tree-hugging, squirrel-kissing pacifist."

"She argued with the deceased a mere hour before he was killed. I'd be derelict in my duties if I didn't question her."

"Did you question her?"

Jack wadded up the paper napkin and tucked it under his now empty plate. "I did."

It was like pulling teeth to get this man to say anything and I had to quell the urge to kick him in the shin. "And?"

"She said she was with Gavin Baldwin all evening. They went to the lake to throw a rose in the water right about the time of the murder."

"See? She didn't do it."

His smile fell. "I can't find anyone to corroborate her story."

The Young Lovers could. If we could find them. Not that Jack would believe it if I did.

"What about Gavin?"

"That would be convenient, wouldn't it?" Jack replied, his tone grim. "They could alibi each other. Except that I cannot find Gavin Baldwin. I went out to his dairy farm this morning and he wasn't there. No one has seen him since the party."

Oh. That wasn't good. Had Daisy's new beau done something bad? Really, really bad? He didn't seem like the type, frankly, but then I'd married a jerk, so perhaps my judgment regarding people wasn't the greatest. Gavin had seemed like a mild-mannered guy.

"Has anyone tried to call him?" I asked hopefully. "I'm sure he must be around. Somewhere."

"I did try calling his cell phone when no one answered the door at his place. I could hear it ringing inside the house. Wherever he is, he didn't take it with him."

"Did you check the barns? Or the pasture?"

"Yes, and yes. He's disappeared."

"People don't just disappear. Is his car at the house?"

"It is."

"That's weird."

I had an image in my head of Gavin ducking behind the kitchen counter to hide while Jack knocked on the front door.

"I can't disagree. I'm working on getting a judge to sign off on a search warrant for Baldwin's house and property. If he's there, we'll find him."

I looked Jack up and down. "You don't appear to working on anything at the moment."

"I have irons in the fire. It's not easy to get anything done in this town the day after one of your parties. Everyone is hungover."

But not Jack. He was always business, morning to night. Kind of annoying.

"What about Jane? Shouldn't you talk to her, too? Or have you already?"

He drank down the last of his iced tea. "She was easy to locate and readily agreed to talk with me. She should be walking through the front door of the inn any minute now. I'll need your drawing room for privacy."

"You don't want to do this at the station?"

He shook his head. "I don't want to make this too official and scare her off. I want her to be comfortable and relaxed. Well…as relaxed as she can be as one of the suspects in a murder investigation. So can I use the drawing room?"

Jack still didn't know that I could hear every word said in the drawing room from my own apartment. I wasn't planning to tell him, either.

"Absolutely. No problem."

I wanted to hear what Jane had to say for herself.

Chapter Six

THE INN HAS been in my father's family for many generations, so it has been through more than a few renovations. My personal apartment on the first floor was one of those, which meant that a window that had been to the outdoors now resided in the far wall of my walk-in closet, only covered by a curtain. It looked perfectly innocent from the drawing room side.

So I found myself once again crouched in my closet listening to Jack interrogate a murder suspect. I'd done this very same thing the day after the Fall Festival and I felt slightly guilty about it. But only a little. Jack was so closed-mouthed about his investigations and I wanted to hear what Jane had to say. I wasn't going to let him try to pin the murder on one of my friends...again. The last time when he'd suspected Missy was one time too many. Luckily, his suspicions had quickly led him in another direction. Hopefully that would happen again today.

"Please have a seat, Miss Allerton. I just need to ask you a few questions."

"Please call me Jane. I have nothing to hide, Sheriff. You can ask me anything."

The woman sounded quite confident. And innocent. Which didn't help Daisy. I didn't necessarily want Jane Allerton to be guilty either, though. I kind of felt sorry for her, dating Colin and all. Last night, it had sounded like she'd liked him, and he'd broken her heart. At a Valentine's ball. That was some shady behavior.

"I appreciate that. Now why don't we start at the beginning? Can you tell me about your relationship with Colin Aiken? How you met? How long have you known each other?"

There was a loud sigh, probably from Jane. "I met Colin about two months ago through one of those internet dating apps. I'd never tried anything like that before, but my friends kept urging me to. They said I might meet someone special. So I signed up because frankly, I wasn't going to meet anyone any other way. I work far too much and have very little social life."

Modern life wasn't easy to navigate, and romance was even tougher.

"What is it that you do for a living?"

Excellent question, although I wasn't sure what it had to do with the Colin's murder. Shouldn't he be asking her whether she left the party right away? Did she come back? C'mon, Jack. Get to it.

"I'm a physical education teacher and also the cheerleading coach at Deauville High School. My squad is the reigning regional champions. It takes up most of my time."

I remembered reading about Deauville cheerleaders in our local paper. Deauville was a town about twenty minutes away and not much larger than Ravenmist. It had been a big deal in the area when they'd won that regional title.

"I imagine that would. Congratulations on the title. Now, Miss Allerton – I mean, Jane – you said that you met Colin Aiken two months ago through a dating app. How well would you say you knew him?"

"I thought I knew him well," she replied, her tone filled with acid. "But clearly I was wrong. I guess I barely knew him at all."

You never really knew someone even if you think you do. I thought I knew David. I thought I knew my parents, but all three had surprised me.

"How often would you see Mr. Aiken?"

"A few times a week. There wasn't room in my schedule for more."

I did some quick mental arithmetic, which honestly wasn't my strong suit, but luckily it wasn't upper-level ciphering. Twice a week for eight or nine weeks made Jane's total investment in Colin sixteen to eighteen evenings. Not much. And she'd truly thought she knew him? That was practically no time at all.

Jack must have done the same calculations because I could hear him nervously clearing his throat.

"Did you ever go to Mr. Aiken's home?"

"His home is being renovated so we mostly hung out at my place or went out."

Alarm bells went off in my head. I would have been suspicious of any man who didn't let me see where he lived. Renovations, my Aunt Fanny. Did he have...a wife? At this point anything was possible.

"What about his work? Did you ever visit him there?"

"He's a graphic designer so he works out of his home mostly. He owns – I mean he *owned* – his own business."

The home that was so chaotic he couldn't have anyone over.

"Did he ever talk about other friends, family, ex-girlfriends or wives? Maybe enemies? Had he angered a client lately?"

I couldn't imagine making one of my guests so mad that they put an arrow through my heart, but it wasn't out of the question. The world was a strange place.

"He was married once. He did say that. A long time ago to his high school sweetheart. They broke up. He'd said they married too young."

I could hear the faint scratching of Jack's pencil against his paper pad. He was going to find that ex-wife, assuming she even existed in the first place.

"Anyone else? Think hard, Jane, because the most minute detail might be just the fact that we need. What seems unimportant to you might be very important to breaking this case."

Another loud sigh. "He did say that he'd used the dating app quite a bit before meeting me, but he hadn't had any luck."

"That helps. Which dating app was it, by the way?"

Jane named a fairly well-known app that I'd seen commercials for and hadn't been in the least tempted to try. Missy had been bugging me lately about *getting out there again,* but I wasn't interested. She'd even suggested that Jack would be…wait for it…jealous if I dated another man.

And he still hadn't asked the right questions. What was he waiting for? This was all nice and good information but not what we needed to know.

"So getting back to the Valentine's Ball," Jack said, his pencil scratching away at his pad. "You left the party about ten o'clock. Is that correct?"

Finally.

"Yes, I took a cab right after I spoke with you and Colin. He'd driven to the party, so I didn't have a ride home."

"And we can confirm that with the cab company?"

A pause. A long one.

"Yes, Sheriff. Am I being accused of something?"

So much for her open attitude about being asked anything. She was clearly defensive about that taxi ride.

"No," Jack replied smoothly. "My job is to rule out people one by one, and I want to do that for you. I just need to confirm your whereabouts at the time of the murder."

"That's fine, then. Yes, go ahead and give them a call."

Except…depending on how long Jane had waited for the cab she might not be in the clear. Deauville was a thirty-minute drive. Tops. She could have been driven home and then come back in her own car, killed Colin, and then snuck out. She could be guilty as sin.

"When you returned home is there anyone who can confirm that you stayed there?"

That's it, Jack. Now we're getting somewhere.

"I live alone but I did call one of my friends to tell her what a crummy date I'd had."

Jane could have done that from her car. It didn't put her in the clear.

"You shouldn't listen in. It's not polite."

The whisper in my ear was followed by a chilly rush of air across my skin. Terrence.

I raised my finger and held it against my lips and then nodded toward the bedroom. I'd heard enough to know that Jane was still a suspect. At least to me. As quickly as I could, I crawled out of the closet and closed the door behind me. Terrence, my live-in ghost and pal, was standing in the middle of my bedroom with his arms crossed and a disappointed look on his face.

"I wasn't trying to be rude. I just needed to know what they were saying. The sheriff thinks that Daisy might have murdered her ex-boyfriend last night. There's no way she would do that."

"Why don't you just ask the sheriff what he found out?"

"Because he doesn't always like to share," I explained. "He can be stubborn."

"So can you."

"What's your point?"

"Listening in to other people's conversations is rude."

I refrained from pointing out that as a ghost who liked to watch the guests that's what he did every day.

"I'll try not to do it again." Sort of noncommittal but still an acknowledgement that my actions weren't the best. "I don't suppose you saw anything last night?"

Terrence shook his head. "I was watching a movie. *Singing in the Rain* is coming on. Want to watch with me?"

It sounded like the perfect way to kill a few hours until Missy and I went to the lake after dark. To look for the Young Lovers. I had to admit that I was excited at the prospect of possibly seeing them.

Two young people whose love was so strong they were willing to die for it. Now they were spending eternity together. Romantic and oh so tragic.

I wasn't the type to die for love. I didn't even like to be uncomfortable or cold or walk around in wet shoes.

I guess that made me the most unromantic woman in Ravenmist.

TEETH CHATTERING, I wrapped my woolen scarf more closely around my neck and face. It was freezing outside. The kind of cold that crawled into your bones and wouldn't budge without a hot bath, a roaring fireplace, and a cask of brandy delivered by a huge and cuddly Saint Bernard. Like Missy, I wanted to find the Young Lovers, but they'd been under wraps for over a hundred years. Maybe a few more months until spring wasn't out of the question?

"I can't feel my lips."

My voice was muffled behind my scarf, but Missy still heard me. It was quiet – almost too quiet – on the banks of the lake.

"It is not that cold, Tedi. You're being overly dramatic."

Was not.

"I can't feel my toes, either. If I lose them, you're going to feel pretty awful."

"I promise you won't lose your toes. You're such a wimp about the cold. You'd think we were trudging across the Arctic tundra the way you're acting."

"I guess it only *feels* that way, huh?"

"It feels colder because there's no sun," Missy explained as if I was a recalcitrant toddler.

"It is colder because there's no sun."

In fact, there wasn't much light at all. The moon was a mere sliver in the sky, which meant that we'd had to bring flashlights to be able to see two feet in front of our faces. We'd pulled our vehicle as close as we could to the lake, but we still had to hike through a scrub of trees to get to it and I was sure that I was going to trip over a protruding root and break an ankle. I wasn't the most graceful and I'd faceplanted more times than I wanted to remember.

The trees were bare, the sky a charcoal black with a few stars dotted here and there. The only sounds around us were the rustling of branches or the hooting of an owl. Creepy. This was why I generally ghost hunted indoors if possible. We'd investigated a few graveyards over the years, but I can't say that I was thrilled to do it.

And we'd done them in the summertime, for heaven's sake.

Let's get this show on the road before my extremities fall off from the weather.

"So…how do you want to do this? Do we call out to them or something? Do you change over?"

I was convinced that Missy's supernatural power gave her some sort of immunity to the cold, but she swore that wasn't the case.

"I don't want to scare or pressure them," Missy said with a shake to her head. She was also bundle up in her warmest down coat and gloves but for some reason she didn't need a hat or earmuffs. By the time we returned to the vehicle her ears would probably be frozen off. We'd find them in the morning along the trail. Ick. "Let's just call their names. I doubt anyone has done that since they passed on."

I didn't say anything, content to let Missy take the lead on this mission. She stepped forward, closer to the banks of the lake and then called their names loudly. Not a shout, but enough to make me jump slightly in the silence.

"Charles Baker! Amelia Croft!" Missy said again when no one answered. "We just want to speak with you. We want to make sure that you're doing okay. Do you need anything? We're here to help you."

I'd always been suspicious of people who said they only wanted to help me, but hopefully Charles and Amelia weren't as cynical as I was.

"Maybe they're not here," I said after several attempts and no response. "They could move wherever they wanted, right?"

"Yes," Missy admitted with a defeated sigh. "If they had enough energy they could have moved hundreds of miles away, but why? Most spirits don't go far from where they passed on. They stay near family, friends, and familiar places and objects."

"If I jumped in a lake because my family members were jerks, I'm not sure that I'd want to hang around for all of eternity. Just sayin'."

Unless I'd decided to haunt them. That might be fun. But Missy would never let me get away with not crossing over if I went first. She'd march me to that light and push me in. Pretty much just as she'd done tonight. When she wanted to be, Missy was a force of nature.

"That's true. I was just hoping they'd show themselves or give us a sign that they're here."

My friend sounded so defeated and I hated to see her this disappointed.

"We can wait," I offered, despite my numb toes, fingers, and nose. "They might appear. We just have to be more patient."

Missy sighed and shook her head. "No, it's okay. You're freezing to death and they're not going to show themselves. You're right, they could be anywhere. I was just...hoping. Let's get you home and warm. I'll even make you some hot choco-late."

I was going to need something a little stronger than cocoa, but I reluctantly agreed, hating to give up on our goal. It felt so anticlimactic. I'd been ready to see two spirits and but instead we'd found bupkis.

I had just turned on my heel to head back to the car when I saw something out of the corner of my eye. Missy must have seen it as well because she grabbed onto my arm, clutching the material of my jacket and jerking me backward.

"Did you see that?"

Her voice was soft and low, barely audible even in the silence.

"I did. It darted behind a tree." I took a deep breath before speaking again. "Should we go and take a look?"

I didn't have any reason to be afraid of ghosts, especially not two lovelorn teenagers, but whomever or whatever we'd seen might be something or someone else. And not friendly. As Missy had told me once before, spirits after death were pretty much like what they were before. If they weren't nice people alive, they weren't very nice dead, either.

Without answering me, Missy stepped toward the spot that we'd seen move and I followed her, of course, not wanting her to do this alone. We were a team, albeit a cold and discouraged one.

We both stopped in front of the large oak just a few feet from the massive trunk. Missy lifted her hand and showed me her crossed fingers.

"Wish me luck. Here goes nothing."

"Amelia? Charles? Are you there? I'm Missy and this is Tedi. We'd like to help you. Can you show yourself? We're not here to hurt you. We only want to be your friend."

Holding my breath, I waited for a response. Any response, but none came. Only silence as we waited. Then, just as I was ready to give up, a gray figure peeked out from behind the tree.

About my height, long hair and pert nose. Slightly glowing too, and not looking near as corporeal as some of the other ghosts in town. More transparent.

"Amelia?" Missy whispered, her gloved hand clutching mine. "Is that you?"

"How do you know my name?"

We'd found Amelia Croft. But where was Charles?

Chapter Seven

AMELIA CROFT LOOKED young, not nearly old enough to have taken her life over what was probably a teenage crush. Her long hair hung down her back and was pulled back with a ribbon that matched the old-fashioned dress she wore that looked like it would have been perfect for one of those old black and white photos where no one ever smiled. She was, in fact, not smiling at the moment, simply staring at us. One of us needed to say something because it was getting mighty awkward.

"Hello, Amelia," Missy finally said softly. "I'm Missy and this is Tedi. We wanted to find you and see if you needed any help."

"Why would I need help?" Amelia's face swung over to me, her brows pinched together in a frown. "Tedi is a boy's name."

"It's short for Theodosia," I replied automatically. I'd been explaining my nickname for most of my life. "It's nice to meet you, Amelia."

"It's lovely to make your acquaintance as well," Amelia answered formally as if remembering her manners. She'd been dead a long time and probably hadn't thought about them in over a hundred years. "Why are you here? No one comes here and calls out our names."

Um, Amelia didn't sound happy about having her eternity disturbed. How did we explain that we knew her name from *the book*? Missy had sworn to me up and down in the car that she wasn't going to be pushy about crossing over, but that didn't mean that Amelia Croft was going to take this in the friendly we're-just-trying-to-help way that we meant it to be.

"You've been out here for over a hundred years," Missy said. "We thought you might be ready to cross over into the light."

No sugarcoating it. Missy just laid it out there. Probably the best way. Get it out into the open.

Amelia's frown deepened. "Over a hundred years? It's felt so much longer."

That didn't jibe by what I'd been told by Edward, Missy's bookstore ghost. He said that time felt shorter and a little strange.

"It has to have been at least two hundred years," a male voice said loudly from behind us. "Or maybe five hundred."

Whirling around, we both came face to face with the ghost of a young man. He looked almost boyish, with a cowlick on the back of his head and his roundish cheeks. He was wearing an old-fashioned suit and carrying a hat.

"Charles Baker, I presume?"

His gaze rested on me, more curious than anything. "Do I know you, miss? If we've met, I fear that I have forgotten. Do forgive me."

I shook my head. "No, but we sort of know you. You both are famous in Ravenmist."

Charles grinned and clapped his hands together. "Famous? We're famous?"

"Famous for being the back of a horse," Amelia snorted from behind us. I stepped to the side so that I could see both of them at the same time. The young woman had her arms crossed over her chest and a look of utter disdain on her face. "It would seem the good people of Ravenmist know you well, Charles."

Wait, this didn't sound like love. Unless love was way different in the 1800s.

"You never change, Amelia," Charles shot back in an accusing tone. "You never let anyone have any fun. Boring and sad is what you are."

"At least I have a sense of propriety, unlike you."

They might have been young lovers in 1874 but in the present, they couldn't seem to stand each other. How…interesting and bizarre.

"You–"

"Now wait a minute," Missy exclaimed, interrupting whatever Charles had been planning to say back to his beloved. "What's going on here? You're famous for being star-crossed lovers but you sound like you hate each other."

Amelia pointed to Charles. "It's all his fault."

"No, it's hers," Charles argued. "She's completely impossible. She has to have everything her way."

"You're one to talk," the young spirit scoffed. "Who had to

stay right here all these years? It wasn't me."

Who'd have thought that spending over a hundred and fifty years with the same person might breed a few complaints? Maybe I wasn't the most unromantic person in Ravenmist after all.

By the time the young lovers had finished airing over a hundred years of grievances with each other I was officially a popsicle. They'd had a long time to build up resentments and boy, did they ever let them fly when Missy and I asked about them.

Amelia was controlling.

Charles was a know-it-all.

Amelia was boring.

Charles was smug.

Amelia never laughed.

Charles laughed too much.

I won't go into any more detail because I'm sure by now that you get the idea. These two couldn't stand one another and here they were spending the rest of their lives together.

"But you both still stay here together?" I asked as delicately as possible. "I mean, you couldn't separate? There isn't some supernatural force keeping you together, is there?"

Charles looked shocked and Amelia appalled. Apparently, it hadn't occurred to them to not be together. After a hundred years or so they were probably used to each other. It was all they knew now.

"Why would we do that?" the young man asked, his brow furrowed into a frown. "Then we'd both be alone."

"Ravenmist is full of spirits," I explained. "I'm sure you could make friends easily."

"Or you could go into the light," Missy said, elbowing me into the ribs. "Like you should have when you passed on. Then you won't be in-between. I can help you with that."

Charles and Amelia exchanged a glance and then shook their heads.

"I don't think so," Charles said. "We're happy right here."

Except that they weren't. Or maybe they were one of those couples that loved to bicker.

"We're happy right here," Amelia repeated. "We don't need any help."

"The offer is open," Missy replied. "Anytime. Day or night. All you have to do is think about the light and I'll appear. Well...I'll appear in the form of the reaper. Not like this. I'm sure you remember the dark-robed person from when you drowned all those years ago. But it will be me and I'll help you cross over. You really should think about it. Being in-between isn't all it's cracked up to be."

"We remember," Amelia said, taking a step back. "He scared us, so we ran."

"We're not scary at all," Missy protested. "We're here to help you. Honest. We just have a sort of scary costume, but we mean no harm. He wouldn't have hurt you, and I won't, either. You have my word."

They must have believed her because they nodded solemnly. There wasn't much left to say since they'd refused to cross over and that had been our original mission tonight. Neither Missy nor I was qualified to be a relationship counselor, so there wasn't much we could do for them.

"We'll come visit again if you like," Missy offered.

Okay, I guess there was one thing we could do. I hadn't planned on offering that, but it wouldn't be any hardship. Especially if the weather was better.

"That…would be lovely," Amelia finally answered. "It does get lonely from time to time."

Charles opened his mouth – probably to start another argument – but then snapped it shut when I sent him a quelling look. These two really needed to chill out.

I'd almost turned to go when I remembered that Daisy had said she and Gavin were here last night throwing a rose into the lake. Digging my phone out of my pocket, I held it up for Missy.

"Let's see if they remember Daisy. She said she was here last night with Gavin."

I couldn't thumb through my photos with my gloves on, so I had to pull one off which made my fingers even more frozen in place. I was quickly able to find one of Daisy and Missy at Christmastime, and I turned the screen to show Amelia and Charles.

"Do you remember seeing this woman here last night? She

would have been with a man and they were throwing a rose into the lake."

The two spirits stepped close and Amelia leaned down to study the photo. Both shook their heads.

"I don't remember her," Charles said. "But that doesn't mean she wasn't here. There were lots of people here last night, so we kept our distance."

"I did notice a few of the people," Amelia admitted. "I didn't see her, though. There were some kids here too last night. A whole group of them."

It sounded like this was a busy location on Valentine's Day.

"Thank you for checking."

Charles took another step closer and I could feel the energy radiating off of him. "Can I see that again? You have pictures in your pocket."

My cell phone? Yes, it probably would amaze them.

"We've seen them before," Amelia explained, "but not up close."

Once again, I held up the phone but this time for Charles. "It's a phone. You can talk to people on it and also take their picture. You can look things up on it, too. Like maps and things."

What a lame explanation. I also wasn't sure what year the telephone was even invented. They'd passed on in 1874. Did they even know the word?

Charles looked at Missy. "If I cross over, will I have one of these?"

Good question. I waited for her response.

"I'm sorry, Charles, but I honestly don't know. I wish I did but I can't say for sure."

He stepped back from me, but his gaze was still on my phone. I had a strange urge to give it to him but that wouldn't make any sense whatsoever. Who was he going to call?

The silence stretched out until it was weird. There was no way to make a graceful exit. So awkward it would be.

"So Missy and I will come back again soon."

With a wave and a few more polite pleasantries Missy and I tromped back down the path to where we'd parked the car. Neither one of us said a word. I don't know what Missy's excuse was, but I was still processing that the Young Lovers were real, and I'd spoken to them and they found cell phones fascinating. If I lived to be a hundred, I'd never get used to meeting new spirits. It was cool, surreal, and strange all at the same time.

I considered myself a fortunate person to be able to interact with them. Even the arguing ones.

When our vehicle came into sight at the edge of the trees, I had to stifle a groan. Jack's official SUV was parked next to it and he was walking around our car, peering into the windows with a flashlight. Darn it all. He was going to wonder what in the heck we were doing out here in the freezing cold.

Missy's eyes were round when she saw him. "The sheriff is here."

"And he's going to be nosy. We better think of a good story. Quick."

Because Jack had an excellent nonsense-detector. He must have honed it working in Chicago as a cop.

At the sound of our footsteps he turned, blasting his flashlight directly into our eyes and almost blinded us. We put up our arms in defense, yelling at him to turn the blasted light off. He didn't but he did point it at the ground.

"What on God's green earth are you two doing skulking around the woods at night?" he asked in an accusing tone. "When I saw your car parked on the side of the road and you nowhere in sight, I was worried sick. I thought I was going to have to call out the dogs to find you."

I still hadn't thought of a decent cover story.

"We were taking a walk."

Missy elbowed me in the ribs. Again. I was going to have bruises after this.

"A walk?" Jack echoed. "On one of the coldest nights of winter? In the dark? Have you lost your minds?"

"Actually," Missy replied, loudly and confidently. "We were ghost hunting the Young Lovers."

That was pretty much the truth, but I didn't think he was going to take that explanation any better than my lame one.

"You couldn't do that in July? It's freezing out here. You could die of hypothermia or get frostbite. Do neither of you have a lick of sense?" The flashlight moved from me to Missy and then back again. "Was this your idea, Tedi?"

He sounded disappointed. Like he thought better of me and I'd let him down. I hadn't meant to.

Missy stepped forward. "Not at all. I convinced Tedi to come with me. It was all my idea, Sheriff. I am sorry if we worried you. It wasn't our intention. We just came up to do some ghost hunting."

That apology seemed to satisfy him, because his shoulders relaxed and he smiled slightly. "I don't have to ask if you found them. Now you need to get home before you both catch pneumonia. And the next time you think about ghost hunting in the middle of nowhere when it's cold, please decide to wait until the spring. Seriously, something bad could have happened. Cell phones don't work out here."

"Sorry, Jack," I murmured, brushing past him to the passenger side of the car. "We really didn't mean any harm."

"I'm just glad it all turned out okay. Another dead body is the last thing we need in Ravenmist."

I wholeheartedly agreed. But in the euphoria of finding the Young Lovers I couldn't help but be reminded that the last dead body in Ravenmist was still on the run. We needed to find Colin Aiken and help him cross over. Where on earth could he be hiding? Missy had looked everywhere for him.

There was something else strange about this night as well...

"Jack, what were you doing out here?"

Chapter Eight

I MANAGED TO thaw out and get some sleep eventually. My mind was buzzing about the entire day – the murder, the young lovers, and then Jack clearly lying to me as to why he was driving around on the edge of town in the middle of the night. When I'd asked him the question, he'd stammered for a moment and then said he was on duty and patrolling.

Hogwash. He'd worked half the night and then all day. No way was the head lawman in Ravenmist on patrol duty later as well. I know what you're thinking...maybe one of his deputies was still hungover or had the crud. That could very well be true, but Jack had part-time backup deputies that loved getting the extra pay every now and then. It was one of the first things he'd done as sheriff, setting up that system. Unless there was a flu plague in town that I hadn't heard of there was no reason for him to be working.

The question was still bothering me the next morning when I swung into Daisy's diner for breakfast and to see how she was doing. I'd stopped by briefly the day before, but she hadn't been there, leaving the restaurant to be run by her assistant. Hopefully, I'd get to talk to her today. According to the town gossip, she'd given her statement to Jack, but she had to be wondering about Gavin and why he'd disappeared.

Missy was already at the table and it looked like she'd ordered my coffee. Thank goodness. I hadn't had time to grab a cup before I left the inn.

I slid into the booth and took a sip of the dark elixir. Heaven in a mug. "Is she here?"

"She is," Missy said, nodding toward the kitchen. "But she hasn't come over to say hi or anything. Maybe she doesn't want to talk about it."

"I don't want to force her to do anything," I assured my friend. "I just want to make sure she's okay. I'm worried about her, with Colin being dead and now Gavin taking a powder. She has worse taste in men than I do."

"Let's not get crazy," Missy laughed. "That would be pretty bad."

I playful stuck out my tongue. "My taste has improved."

"How would we know? You never date. Neither does the sheriff, by the way. Maybe you could—"

"Stop right there," I warned her. "You don't have to say it. I could do worse, right? That's what everyone says."

"I'm only saying that you two looked very nice together at the ball when you were dancing."

"That's not the greatest criteria for a relationship."

"It's a start. Now what are you going to order?"

"Waffles," I answered immediately. I might not have been

able to figure out why Jack was lying to us, but I had decided what to put in my empty stomach. "With a side of ham."

Because as my father always said, if something is worth doing it's worth doing well.

The waitress came and took our order while Daisy seemed to find several reasons not to travel into the vicinity of our table. She constantly went back into the kitchen, only coming out to the dining room on a rare occasion. I wasn't stupid. She didn't want to talk to us. Or maybe just me. Either way, she was avoiding us, and I had to be good with it. Only it made me worry all the more. She wasn't smiling, and she didn't have the usual zip in her step.

After tucking away two waffles, I excused myself from the table and headed to the ladies' room to freshen up my lipstick. I was still digging in my purse for the gold tube when the door swung open and Daisy walked in.

"I've been wanting to talk to you."

That was a surprise considering she hadn't looked me in the eye for the last forty-five minutes, but I wasn't going to quibble.

"I wanted to talk to you, too. I've been so worried about you."

Daisy wasn't a hugger, so I wasn't quite prepared when she reached out and pulled me into a tight, almost desperate hug. "Heavens, Tedi, I'm not sure what to do or who to turn to. I think the sheriff thinks I did it."

Patting her on the shoulder, I shook my head. "There is no way he could think that. Everyone in town knows that you wouldn't hurt a fly. Besides, I would think that Gavin would be his major suspect right now. And Jane too, of course."

Daisy's eyes welled up with tears. "I can't believe that it would be Gavin. He would never do something like that. He's a gentle man."

"Do you know where he is? If you do, you should tell the sheriff. This doesn't look good for him."

"I really don't," she vowed. "I'm worried about him, too. This is so unlike him."

I wanted to believe that. It was a jerk move to disappear and leave Daisy facing the music, but that was only my humble opinion. It didn't endear me to Gavin at the moment.

"I'm sure it is," I said instead. "But you can't think of any-where that he might be? Think hard. Someplace he might have mentioned in a conversation? Maybe a friend he likes to visit?"

Daisy sighed, wringing her hands together. "He doesn't talk about himself much. Sort of the strong, silent type. When he does talk, we talk about the farm or the restaurant or music or movies. He's never mentioned anything outside of Ravenmist."

"He must have. He hasn't lived here all of this life. Where did he grow up?"

Daisy opened her mouth to answer but then stopped, her eyes growing round. "I–I don't know."

"Did you ever talk about your childhoods?"

"We did. I told him about mine and then…"

"And then," I prompted when she didn't continue. "What did he say?"

"I don't remember," she confessed, a stunned look on her

face. "If he said anything, I don't remember."

Maybe Gavin was some sort of hypnotist and could make people forget things and cluck like a chicken. My parents had taken me and my sisters to see one when we were kids.

"It's probably just the trauma of all that's happened," I assured her with another awkward hug. "You'll remember eventually. In the meantime, is there anything I can do for you? Anything at all."

It was a rather rash offer, but Daisy had always been someone the entire town could count on.

"I'm fine. Honest. It's just all so sad and scary. I didn't want to date Colin anymore, but I didn't want him dead, either."

"Do you know of anyone who might want him dead? Did he have enemies?"

"He never talked about that. He only bragged about all the friends he had. Important people, he said. Wealthy and powerful."

"Did you give the sheriff any names of his friends? He might need to talk to them."

"I did." She wrinkled her nose in distaste. "He asked about any old girlfriends, but Colin never mentioned any by name. He only said that he'd broken a few hearts over the years."

I didn't like to think ill of the dead, so I pushed my unkind thoughts to back of my brain. Whatever Colin Aiken may have done in life, he didn't deserve to be killed for it.

"So you'd never seen Jane before the other night?"

"Never. I had no idea about her." Her lips drooped, and she sighed heavily again. "But I knew he was seeing other women.

He was cad, wasn't he? Why couldn't I see it at the beginning?"

"Because you like to see the best in people. It's one of your most wonderful qualities."

"I feel so stupid," she whispered, her head hanging. "Like an old fool."

"You figured out what he was and you dumped him. Seems like you were the smart one. Not foolish at all. Don't give yourself a hard time about this, Daisy. Men like Colin Aiken come and go in a woman's life. They've practiced all the lines and know how to deliver them. Even the smartest female can be taken in, especially if they have a good and loving heart. They take advantage of that."

Sniffling, Daisy wiped her eyes with her apron. "I just feel so stupid. About Colin. About Gavin. About...everything. I'm supposed to have psychic abilities. I sure didn't see any of this coming."

"You're not stupid. At least you didn't marry them. I had to do that to figure out David was a creep."

Daisy tried to smile as she dabbed at her damp cheeks. "There's that, I suppose. I'm just worried the sheriff is going to come after me, Tedi. What if he does?"

"Then we'll make sure he finds the real killer. Just like we did when he thought Missy was a suspect last fall. But I think he's a pretty good cop, actually. You don't even have a decent motive. You'd already broke up with Colin and had moved on. Why kill him? It doesn't make any sense. Jack will know better."

At least I hoped so.

Chapter Nine

AFTER BREAKFAST, I was still wondering about others that might want Colin dead when I walked by the corner coffee shop and saw my father sitting at a table by the front window. Not alone. He was with the woman he'd escorted to the Valentine's Ball and he appeared to be having a wonderful time, his head thrown back in laughter. What was her name? Kate. Kate-something with a B.

I tried to bustle by without being seen but my luck was running thin this morning and he spied me, waving happily and motioning to me to join them. There was no polite way to refuse and I felt terrible that it even crossed my mind. I was quite close to my both of my parents and avoiding them wasn't an act that came naturally to me. I genuinely enjoyed their company but since they'd announced their impending divorce, I admit that I'd spent less time with them.

I wasn't sure that I would ever get used to seeing either of them with anyone else. I was going to have to find a way, however, as they didn't look to be getting back together. I'd had hope in the beginning but after all this time it probably wasn't going to happen.

"Hey, Dad." I leaned down to kiss his cheek and give Kate a small smile. As much as I wished she wasn't sitting there all of this wasn't her fault. She seemed like a nice person from what I could tell. "How are you today?"

"I'm fine, pumpkin. Why don't you sit down? I'll order you a hot chocolate, extra whipped cream."

My dad knew my weaknesses and whipped cream was one of them. But...

"I wish I could, but I really need to be getting back. Plus, I met Missy at Daisy's this morning and I'm stuffed like a turkey. I couldn't eat or drink another bite."

Dad laughed, the lines around his eyes crinkling. I was again reminded that my parents weren't that old. They still had a great deal of living to do and I wanted them to enjoy it.

He looked really happy. Was it because of this woman sitting next to him? She looked happy, too.

"Let me guess. Waffles?" He didn't give me a chance to answer. "Do you remember Kate Beckswith from the ball?"

"I do remember. It's lovely to see you again, Kate."

I shook Kate's hand and had a chance to take another look at her. Neat and trim, she was dressed in casual blue jeans and a cream and brown sweater. She was certainly attractive.

"It's lovely to see you, too," she replied with a kind smile. "I wanted to tell you what an amazing party it was the other night. The food and decorations were wonderful. You should be very proud."

I was but it was always nice to hear kind words.

"Thank you. I'm glad you had a good time."

Neither one of us mentioned the unfortunate murder. I hoped she didn't think that dead bodies hanging around the inn were a common occurrence.

Kate stood and my dad hopped to his feet as well. "I wish I could stay but I do have to run. I'm volunteering at the county hospital today and if I don't leave now I'll be late. I'm still getting used to driving in the snow again. Thank you for the coffee and Danish, Dan."

"Thanks for meeting me." My dad leaned down and gave Kate a peck on the cheek. "I'll call you later, okay?"

"Sounds perfect."

With my dad's help, Kate shrugged into her down coat and she waved as she headed out the door. That left me and my dad and an awkward silence. I simply wasn't sure what I was supposed to say.

"So I guess I should be getting to the inn—"

"Stay a minute," my dad said. He didn't make it sound like an option. "I think we need to talk."

When Daniel Hamilton said that *we* needed to talk, what he really meant was that *he* was going to talk and *I* was going to listen. Images of my teenage years passed before my eyes and I sank down into my chair without a protest. It would be faster and easier to simply go with it and get it over with.

Without consulting me, he ordered the hot chocolate that I had refused and it was slid before me without much fanfare a short time later. Mounded with whipped cream. If forced to drink it, I was going to enjoy every decadent, sugar-filled sip.

Let's get the show on the road. Neither one of us was getting any younger.

"So what did you want to talk about?"

As if I didn't know.

"We could start with your attitude."

How many times had we discussed that very topic when I was in junior high and high school? Too many times to count.

Apparently, it hadn't done any good but I wasn't going to point that out at the moment.

There were many ways to deal with Dan Hamilton when he was in this mood and I decided to play dumb. He might even buy into it.

"I don't know what you mean."

"I think you do." He tapped the table with his index finger, a sure sign he was annoyed. "I like Kate and I want you to be polite to her."

"You don't think I was polite?"

He rolled his eyes, a move that I had reserved strictly for myself. "You were polite, but you weren't, you know, really polite. You were stiff, like it was forced."

"I didn't mean to be. I'm sorry. I'll apologize to her if you like."

Short answers. Don't elaborate. I'd learned early in my youth. Don't apologize too much or he'd wonder what else I'd been up to. And don't ever offer any information. Dad was the master of acting like he knew something when he didn't know anything at all but suddenly you were apologizing for something you never didit.

"That's not necessary but I'd like you to be a little warmer next time you and she meet. She's a wonderful woman, Tedi, and I think you'd get along if you gave her a chance."

And I'd be a terrible person not to. I knew that.

"Of course, I'll give her a chance."

"I know this is a lot for you to get used to, pumpkin."

"It is."

I couldn't argue with his statement.

"Your mother and I tried to make it work for a long time but eventually we realized that it wasn't going to. I know you blame your mom for the divorce, but I can assure you that it was just as much my idea as hers." He rubbed his chin and smiled. "We're happier now. Both of us. We'll always care about each other, but we simply don't want to be married anymore. It doesn't have anything to do with you girls. It's us."

I didn't want to be the party pooper in my parents' lives. I'd do better. Starting now.

I took a deep breath and gathered my courage. In for a penny, in for a pound as the saying goes. "You should bring Kate by the inn one night for dinner. I'd like to get to know her better."

Dad grinned like a kid on Christmas morning and my heart squeezed. I needed to keep my own emotions out of this situation. It wasn't about me.

I'd repeat that over and over until it sunk in.

"Pumpkin, there's nothing I'd like better. I think you and Kate will get on like a house afire. She's really terrific."

"How did you meet her?"

Images of a smoky bar or worse…an online dating app made me shudder.

"I've known Kate for years. She was my high school girl-friend, but we broke up after graduation. Different colleges and all of that stuff. She's lived in Ocala, Florida until recently. Her husband owned a horse farm there, but he died a few years ago. She sold it and decided to move back home to be closer to her sister and brother. We ran into each other at the grocery store and well…we kind of got to talking…"

That explained why Kate was nervous about driving in the snow. She'd lived in Florida. And she was a widow. And also, my dad's old girlfriend. It was weird to think of him before he met my mom in college. Wait…

"I remember seeing your senior prom picture. Was that Kate?"

My dad had worn a powder blue tux with a ruffled shirt and his date had been sporting a Farrah Fawcett hairdo. Got to love the seventies.

"It was. She's hardly changed at all."

There was a gleam in my dad's eye that told me he wasn't sitting with me in the corner coffee shop. He was in the past wearing his boogie shoes and polyester shirt.

"Just pick a night and we'll have dinner." I screwed up my nose as I remembered that I had a prior commitment that night.

"Except for tonight. We're supposed to be doing an investigation at The Raven's Wing Pub. They're closing early for us. How about tomorrow evening?"

"I'll check with Kate but that sounds great. Just give her a chance, pumpkin. That's all I ask."

"I will, Dad. I promise."

That was a promise I intended to keep.

Chapter Ten

THE RAVEN'S WING Pub was located on the north edge of town and according to records was over a hundred and fifty years old. It served bar food and drinks to patrons over the legal age and was a favorite place amongst the townsfolk to watch sporting events. It was also purported to be incredibly haunted. The customers and employees all had stories, but we'd investigated the place twice since I'd moved home and we'd never come across anything close to supernatural.

That was, of course, before the mysterious surge of energy in Ravenmist that was making the long quiet spirits get up and party. Literally. I had high hopes that tonight we'd see an actual ghost.

Our two tech geeks, Elliott and Lloyd Farraday had set up all of the equipment and we were ready to roll by ten o'clock. As usual Missy and I were there along with Harold Pine, the mayor, and Mary Eckley, a retired history teacher that now ran a small antique shop in the downtown area. Jack was there as well with his teenage son Tyler who was dying to see his first ghost. They'd come to every single investigation since joining the association and I had to admire their dedication, especially as so many of these events were held on a school night. Business didn't want to close early on a weekend.

The pub was a four-story structure if you counted the dusty, decrepit basement. While I hadn't yet seen a ghost at The Raven's Wing I'd felt totally creeped out both times that we were here, constantly looking over my shoulder. I'd been sure that someone was staring at me. Now that I knew ghosts were real, I was positive that indeed someone had been staring at me. So rude.

The first two floors of the pub were open to the public. The second story was actually more of a loft area that the owners had turned into television central. On any given Sunday in the fall, a customer could watch every single football game in the country by simply swiveling their chair.

The third floor was used for storage and an office area, so it also scored high on the creep factor scale. Dark, deserted, and with rows and rows of shelves that an axe murderer could hide behind.

Did I mention that I could be a tad dramatic at times? I watch too many movies. The top floor, however, was the only decent place for us to set up our monitors. I'd stuck close to the door.

Elliott and Lloyd headed straight to the basement to investigate and Missy volunteered to watch the monitors. Harold and Mary went down the back stairs to the detached garage where a waitress said she saw a full body apparition sitting in the passenger seat of her car. She'd screamed and it disappeared.

"I can watch with you," I offered. "Jack, you and Tyler can do the main pub if you like."

Tyler almost jumped out of his seat with excitement but was pushed back down into the chair by his father's hand on his shoulder.

"Just a second, son. Remember we talked about this. You can't do the fun stuff and not do the work. Last time you didn't take one turn at the monitors."

The excited smile fell from Tyler's face only to be replaced by defeated resignation.

"Dad," he groaned. "I will, I promise."

"I know you will because you're going to do it right now. You can help Missy. Tedi and I will take the first turn in the pub."

How did this happen? I hadn't been paying close enough attention and now I was going to be ghost hunting with Jack. A man who didn't believe in the slightest and was basically humoring his son. And me. And Missy. And Elliott, Lloyd, Harold, and Mary. Pretty much the entire population of Ravenmist.

I gave Missy a look that begged for help but she only chuckled and grinned. She wouldn't be any assistance. I was stuck.

Grabbing my flashlight, I heaved a heavy sigh. "Okay, let's do this then."

Jack knew the rules by now, so neither one of us said anything as we descended the stairs and began walking through the quiet loft area. I'd done many of these investigations, but it was always weird to be in a public building that was usually bustling with noise and people only to see it dark and deserted.

We settled at a table that had an amazing view of both the loft and the downstairs. I placed the voice recorder on the table and began asking the usual questions with long pauses between. Jack sat back and crossed his legs, studying the bar against the far wall and completely ignoring me. I was fine with it.

We'd been down there for quite awhile and I was getting antsy to move. I hadn't seen or heard anything, and I was anxious to hear if the others had any luck. I was just about to call it quits and go back upstairs when I saw a movement out of the corner of my eye. On the first floor, near the fire exit. Peering over the railing of the loft, I moved the beam of my flashlight slowly from side to side, trying to illuminate the area.

That's when I saw him. He was standing by a table near the restrooms. Faint but distinguishable. And thankfully just out the line of sight from our camera.

Colin Aiken. Or at least the ghost of him.

I needed to tell Missy as soon as possible. Tossing a glance over my shoulder, I saw that Jack was still studying the bar. Thank goodness. He didn't need to know about any of this. But of course, he chose that particular moment to be interested in what I was doing.

"Do you see something?"

I snapped off my flashlight and sat back down in my chair, hoping I appeared casual and nonchalant. "Nope. Nothing at all.

In fact, I think we should call it quits and go upstairs."

Without a word of argument – for once – Jack led the way back to the top floor while I practically vibrated with excitement behind him. All we had to do was talk to Colin and get him to cross over into the light. But first, I needed to ask him one tiny question.

Do you know who killed you?

IT WASN'T EASY to alert Missy as to who I'd seen without also arousing the suspicion of Jack, who was currently peering closely at the monitor because Tyler had excitedly told him that there'd been a moving shadow on the first floor of the pub. Probably Colin. Because he was a new spirit, he didn't have much energy. Thankfully, Jack was busy giving his son all the normal, everyday reasons there could be for seeing a shadow on video. Sometimes his skeptical nature came in handy.

As much as I wanted Tyler to see a ghost, I wasn't sure that seeing a recently deceased one was the best idea. I'd been hoping for a spirit that was almost as old as the building but instead I'd been given a slick ladies' man who didn't want to cross over.

"Missy and I will go downstairs and check," I said, leaning as casually as I could against the doorway and silently praying that Colin would stay out of sight. "Why don't you two head to the basement? That's where most of the reports come from."

I didn't need to say it twice. Tyler practically bounded out of his chair with his dad on his heels. They stomped down the back staircase that went directly to the basement. The teenager made so much noise that if there were any spirits in the vicinity, they were probably in hiding now.

I grabbed Missy's arm and tugged her toward the doorway. She was still in the dark as to what was going on. "Let's go. You need to see this."

"What?" she asked in a hushed tone as we descended the staircase. "You're acting strange."

He was there, still standing by the table. I pointed to Colin. "He's here. We need to talk to him."

I could hear Missy suck in a breath and before I could react, she was walking briskly across the room to where he stood. When she reached him she leaned closer and said something. I was afraid he was going to run again but he only nodded and followed her into the dark corridor that led to the restrooms.

I wasn't sure what I should do. Follow or stay here? Crossing over seemed like a personal moment in life and I didn't want to crash the party. But I'd be a liar if I said that I wasn't curious. Besides, I needed to ask him if he'd seen his killer. Decision made, I hurried into the corridor only to find it deserted. Where were they?

A cursory inspection of the ladies' room revealed that Missy had moved him there. The two of them were having a quiet but earnest conversation so I hesitated in the doorway until they'd finished. Finally, Missy turned to me and smiled.

"He's ready to move on. I told him you wanted to talk to

him first."

He didn't look happy about it. If anything, he appeared to be frightened, wringing his hands together and shifting from foot to foot.

"Thank you for talking to me, Colin."

"It's okay. It's fine."

"I'm sorry about what happened to you. You're…ready to go into the light now?"

He nodded. "I don't like the in between. I ran because I was scared but this is far worse. I don't know anyone, and it all feels so strange. I just want peace."

I didn't know where Colin was headed but Missy had assured me that the vast majority did, indeed, find that elusive peace.

"I just wanted to ask you if you could help us find whomever did this to you. Do you remember anything about that night? Colin, do you remember who killed you?"

He straightened then, his shoulders squaring and his chin lifting defiantly. "I do remember. It was Daisy. She killed me."

This was bad. So very, very bad.

Chapter Eleven

"DAISY WOULD NEVER hurt anyone."

I said it with conviction because I deeply believed it. There was no way she could have killed Colin. Not Daisy. She didn't even like to step on ants.

"It was her." Colin sounded indignant. "I know she did it."

Missy – who at some point had turned into her Reaper persona when I wasn't paying any attention – tried to play mediator. "Let's all keep calm here. I'm sure there's a reasonable explanation."

"There is. She killed me."

As a circle of light bloomed in the corner of the room, it seemed to sap Colin's energy. He faded until he was almost nothing but a wisp of gray, barely visible and a little fuzzy. The light grew and shone from the ceiling to the floor like a spotlight on a big stage.

This was seriously freaky.

"Start from the beginning, Colin," Missy commanded. I couldn't see her face because of the black hood but her voice was bossy enough that he complied.

"I didn't leave the party right away even though the sheriff told me to. I hung around for awhile. It was a party and I'd paid to be there, so why not have some fun?."

I couldn't stop my mouth from opening and speaking out loud.

"Because you'd just broken your girlfriend Jane's heart, maybe?"

"She knew it wasn't serious. She acted all heartbroken, but I'd told her in the beginning that I wasn't looking for anything long-term. Just casual."

He might have told her that, he might not. At this point it was he said, she said. Of course, Colin lacked credibility since he'd lied to Daisy and who knows how many others.

"So you stayed…" Missy prompted as the light in the corner grew brighter. I had to squint to be able to see Colin's faint outline. "What happened then?"

"I stopped at the buffet, then went outside for some fresh air. That's when it happened."

We both waited to hear what *it* was.

"I walked over to the gazebo to smoke a cigarette. It was deserted so I smoked my cigarette as fast as I could because it was freezing out there. Just as I was finishing up, I heard footsteps and turned around, I saw Daisy in the distance standing on the back deck and leaning over the railing. She seemed to be looking for something or someone. I guess she was looking for me. Anyway, I turned back to throw out my cigarette and I heard footsteps again. Only this time closer."

For a guy that was about to go into the light he was incredibly dramatic, drawing out the story. He needed to just get to it.

"And? What happened then?" I pressed. "Did you turn and see Daisy?"

"I didn't have time. I turned and immediately the arrow went into my chest. I died pretty quickly."

Missy was frowning, and I had a feeling that I was wearing a matching expression.

"Why do you think Daisy did it then?" I demanded, hands on hips. "You don't know for sure. You didn't see anything."

"I saw her right before I died," he argued, his outline completely disappearing. He was nothing but a voice now. "It had to be her. I didn't see anyone else."

"You can't make that sort of jump in logic," I replied testily. Accusing someone of murder was no joke. "She could have gone back inside. She could have done many things. It isn't a slam dunk that she was the one that shot you. And I can guarantee you that she wasn't looking for you either."

"All I know is that I saw her and then I was dead. That's good enough for me."

"It won't be for a court of law," I argued. "What motive would she have? You were broken up and she'd moved on."

Missy nodded in agreement. "Tedi makes a good point."

Of course, I did.

"She had reason. Why don't you ask her about it?"

I didn't have time to reply that I would ask her. The next thing I knew the spotlight curled up on itself and then disappeared into the ceiling, leaving Missy and I standing in the dark. She reached over to the wall switch and flipped on the light, already changed back into her regular persona. Just Missy.

I turned and looked around the room. Where was Colin? "What happened?"

"He's moved on."

Such simple words but they had a major impact.

"He can't have yet. He didn't say why Daisy would want him dead."

"No, he didn't. We'll have to ask her."

I would. First thing in the morning.

"There's no way she did it, Missy. He can't be right."

"I'm sure he's not but we do need to talk about this with her. We have to tell her what Colin said."

That meant telling Daisy about a whole lot of things. Including Missy's fun little hobby of escorting souls to the afterlife. And then there was Jack...

Thank goodness he would never believe that Colin's ghost told them that the killer was Daisy.

STILL IN SOMEWHAT of a daze after the encounter with Colin, I stumbled back up the stairs to the top floor. I tried to act calm, cool, and collected but inside I had a mass of churning lava in my gut. Colin had basically thrown Daisy under the bus and then jumped into the light without giving any more details. He said she had motive for killing him and of course my brain was whirling with possible ideas, but I'd discarded them one by one. I couldn't think of anything that would turn Daisy into a cold-blooded killer.

Harold and Mary were manning the monitors while Elliott and Lloyd investigated the perimeter of the building and the garage. Tyler was slumped in a chair tapping on his phone and Jack was standing in a far corner talking into his cell. From the look on his face, it was a business call. He had that earnest, focused look that I'd come to know and sort of tolerate. After a few minutes he finished his call and strode over to me as I was winding up a long extension cord. It was time to break down for the evening.

"Let Tyler and I do that." Jack tapped his son on the shoulder and the teenager groaned and rolled his eyes. "Let's get to work so we can get you home and in bed. You have school tomorrow."

"I'm not tired."

"I am," Jack declared. "So let's get to work so I can go to bed. I have to be up early in the morning."

Tyler was really a good kid and he didn't complain anymore, simply pitching in and doing what needed to be done. Like so many other nights, we packed the Farraday van with equipment. The men would store it in their basement until the next investigation. It always seemed to be me and Jack in the parking lot at the end of the night and this was no exception. Tyler was in the back seat of Jack's SUV with the heater on, once again texting on his phone while we stood beside my vehicle.

Freezing to death. What was it about my friends that made them want to see me shiver? I needed to find out why and if they were all in league to torture me.

"What's happening in the morning?"

Jack frowned, looking confused. "Pardon?"

"You told Tyler that you needed to be up early in the morning. What's going on? Do you have a line on where Gavin might be?"

His disappearance made him mighty suspicious to me, no matter what Colin had said before he crossed over.

"Maybe I'm just anxious to have a bear claw at the coffee shop."

It was my turn to roll my eyes. "Try again. You're more of a bran muffin kind of guy."

"Ouch. Now that hurt, Tedi. I like bear claws." Rubbing his chin, Jack glanced into the back seat of his vehicle where his son was blissfully playing on his phone. "Actually, that last call I took was from a buddy of mine at the Chicago PD. He checked out Colin Aiken for me."

"And?"

It would be just like Jack to bring up the subject and then refuse to talk about it.

"He told me some interesting tidbits."

He was such a tease.

"There's a croissant breakfast sandwich in it for you tomorrow morning if you share."

"With grilled ham?"

"How are you not four hundred pounds? Fine, with grilled ham."

"I have a fast metabolism. I might as well tell you because it will be all over town before lunch." Jack rested a hand on the roof of my car and leaned down as if telling me a huge secret. "It seems our victim didn't run his own graphic design company. That was a story he told Jane. His business dealings were vague at best and always shady, sort of under the radar. From what my friend found out, Colin Aiken was mostly a fraud and a con man."

"I wish I were surprised."

"There's more if you want to hear it."

More teasing. More delays.

"I'm tired, Jack. And cranky. Cranky enough to tell my chef to never fix you another meal."

"I think that's an idle threat but just in case I will tell you. It seems that Aiken was an avid user of that dating app where he met his girlfriend Jane. He dated many women that he met there, and some of them were not single. There might be a few pissed-off husbands that have motive to want Aiken dead."

Now we were getting somewhere. And it was far away from Daisy too, which was even better.

"So you'll check them out?"

Jack nodded. "But that's not the most interesting thing my friend told me. Aiken was also married."

No...wait. Married?

"As in not single? He told Jane he was divorced."

"They never bothered to get a divorce. He did marry young and they're still legally married. They don't live together though, and from what my friend can tell they've been living separate lives for years. She's a surgeon in Miami." He held up his hands when I opened my mouth to ask a question. "And before you say anything, she has an airtight alibi. She was operating on the victim of a three car pileup at the time of death. She's coming up to Illinois to see about selling his home and packing up his possessions."

Colin Aiken was a big old liar and I had no reason to believe what he'd said about Daisy. That had probably been another one of his stories.

But I'd better talk to her just to be sure.

Chapter Twelve

THE NEXT MORNING I was up with the birds, despite a lousy night's sleep. My mind was far too busy cogitating over the entire evening at the Raven's Wing. Daisy, Colin, and whatever he might know that she wouldn't want public. If it was even true. It was settled fact that Colin Aiken had a casual relationship with the truth.

"You look in a hurry."

Terrence lounged against the bathroom doorway watching me apply my lipstick. I had a long list of things to do today and at the top was a visit to Daisy's.

"That's because I am in a hurry. My work is never done. What are your plans today?"

"An Elizabeth Taylor movie marathon. It's starts with *National Velvet.*"

I'd seen that movie years ago as a child. I think Mickey Rooney was in it as well, but I wasn't sure. It had been too long.

"Enjoy it. I'll be in and out all day, plus I'll be having dinner with my dad and his girlfriend in the dining room tonight."

Many nights Terrence and I hung out in front of the television and ate dinner. Well, I ate dinner and he watched television. I didn't want him to worry about where I was.

"If you're done by nine the finals of that cooking show are on tonight."

Ohhhh, I did want to see that.

"I'll try," I vowed. "We're eating at seven, so we should be done by then."

"You're never here anymore."

That wasn't the complete truth. I was at the inn quite a bit, but I wasn't spending as much time in my little apartment lately. No one loved curling up on the couch more than I did but it seemed like I had a million things that needed to be done and little time to do them.

"I'll be home more from here on out. This is our slow time until the spring."

It was kind of sweet that he missed me, though.

Terrence shook his head. "That's not what I mean. Even when you're here, you're not really here. Your head is someplace else. Is it that sheriff?"

"Heavens to Betsy, no. He's just a friend."

"You spend an awful lot of time with him."

Did I? I hadn't been keeping track. Apparently, Terrence was.

"No more than I spend with Missy."

I was sure that I spent more time with her. No question about that.

"If you and he got married, would he move in here?"

Whoa. Hold the gosh darn phone. Was this the bee in Terrence's bonnet this morning? Was he worried about what would happen to him if I ever had a man in my life?

Shoving the gold tube of lipstick into my purse, I faced my closet-ghost head on. I wanted him to see my expression and know that I was telling the absolute, one hundred percent truth.

"Jack and I are just friends. Really. But even if we were more – which let me repeat that we are not – you would always have a home here. Always."

"So you would tell him about me?"

Sighing, I grappled with that question. "Technically he already knows about you. He saw you that night, but it seems he's blocked it out of his mind. He doesn't want to believe in ghosts so he…doesn't."

Jack had a special brand of denial that I couldn't help admiring. It was as if that night had never happened. Complete erasure from his brain cells. It was a cute party trick that I'd love to emulate.

"I'm not planning to ever get married again," I declared firmly. "I'm happy being single."

Terrence contemplated my words for a few long moments and then seemed satisfied with my answer.

"I like it here."

"I'm really glad. I like having you here."

Even if I had to dress in the bathroom.

He began to fade, his outline growing fuzzier with each second. "I'll see you later, Tedi. Keep warm."

Lipstick applied, I dashed out of the inn and down the block toward Daisy's. The restaurant was busy at this time of the morning, and the smell of freshly ground coffee and bacon wafted around my nose. I sniffed the air appreciatively and my stomach growled in anticipation. I wasn't here for breakfast, but a few pancakes wouldn't hurt, right? A girl has to eat.

I was halfway through a shortstack smothered in maple syrup before I was able to flag Daisy down and get her attention. She slid into the booth across from me, her cheeks pink from bustling in and out of the warm kitchen.

"Do you need more coffee?"

Yes, but that wasn't important. Okay, it was important but not as important.

"We need to talk, Daisy." I kept my voice low, although the diner was so loud I doubted anyone would overhear. The breakfast rush was at its peak and it was standing room only. "It's urgent."

She glanced around and then nodded. "Okay, we can go in my office. You can bring your pancakes with you."

My appetite had suddenly vanished as my brain had contemplated the task ahead of me. I was going to have to tell Daisy a few things she might not believe.

"I'm done. Let's go."

Grabbing my half-full cup of joe, I followed Daisy back into her office where it was much more peaceful. I settled onto the small loveseat and took a sip of coffee, stalling for time. How did one go about this? I had no idea. Might as well just go for it.

Daisy settled next to me and folded her hands in her lap. "What did you want to talk about?"

Ghosts. The Grim Reaper. Secrets.

"Would you believe that I spoke with Colin Aiken's ghost?"

There it was. She'd either believe me or call a doctor.

She hesitated for a moment and then eased back on the couch, her body relaxing when I thought she would go tense. "Yes, Tedi. Yes, I would. I've seen some strange things in this town over the years. Where did you see Colin?"

Ooookay… This was looking promising. She didn't think I was a loon.

"At The Raven's Wing last night. Right before he crossed over into the light." I paused, looking for the right words. Did I even need to tell her about Missy? What the heck. Missy had given the green light. "He didn't cross over originally when he died the night of the ball. I know that because Missy is a Reaper. What I mean by that is that she can change into the Grim Reaper and escort the dead into the light. If they wish to go, that is. She can't force them."

I had started to ramble, so I immediately shut my mouth. Daisy wasn't as relaxed as she'd appeared only moments ago, but she hadn't flung herself at the exit, either.

"Missy is the Grim Reaper?"

"One of his helpers. The official Grim Reaper is her uncle."

"The one in Boca?"

"Yes."

So far, so good.

"And you spoke with Colin?"

"I did." Gathering my courage, I pressed forward. "Daisy, he said that you were the last one that he saw before he died. You were out on the deck. He also said that you...had a motive for wanting him dead. He said I should ask you about it."

Her face went white and her hand fluttered up to her throat where a strangled noise had escaped her lips.

"I didn't want him dead."

Daisy's voice was hushed, and I had to lean closer to hear her.

"That's good. I never thought you did," I assured her. "But he seemed to believe that you had motive. What's he talking about?"

Jumping up from the loveseat, Daisy nervously paced the room a few times before stopping in her tracks, turning to face me, and answering.

"I told him something. Something personal. Something that I wouldn't want my sister to know. She's so judgmental. Needless to say, I shouldn't have trusted him."

I'd never met the sister, so I'd have to take Daisy's word for it. I had met Aiken and I could only agree that she'd used poor judgment there. I didn't say anything else or push. If she didn't want to tell me, I had to be fine with that. There was a part of me that wasn't sure I really wanted to know, anyway.

"Jack doesn't know anything about this, Daisy. He wouldn't believe it, of course, even if I did tell him. But if he's going to find out something down the road it might be better for you to tell him yourself."

Gathering my purse, I stood and stepped toward the door. I'd said what I needed to say, and she could do as she pleased with the information. I had my hand on the doorknob when I heard her speak behind me.

"I got caught for shoplifting."

My hand dropped, and I turned to face her. "That doesn't sound like a hanging offense. What happened?"

"I was young," she sighed, her shoulders slumped. "And stupid and hungry. We were in dire straits financially. So I stole some food from a convenience store. I'd done it before and I thought I could get away with it again. But I got caught. The officer took pity on me and let me off with a warning after hearing my story. I swear I never did it again. It scared me straight."

Right there. That explained why Daisy was always feeding the homeless and anyone else who was down on their luck. She was famous for her charitable works in Ravenmist.

"I've tried to make up for what I did—"

"You don't owe anyone an explanation," I interrupted. "If the cop thought you were worthy of only giving a warning then I'm sure that you were. You were desperate and starving, Daisy. It was wrong, and you learned that. I'm sure your sister would understand."

Daisy shuddered and shook her head. "Hyacinth would never understand. She only sees black and white."

That sounded like a difficult way to live life.

"Had Colin threatened to tell Hyacinth about what happened?"

Daisy fell back into a chair with an audible groan. "When I broke up with him, he said that I wasn't any better than he was. He made some remark about wondering what my sister would think. I threw him out then and there and told him not to come back. You saw how effective that was. He showed up here and tried to turn on the charm. I'd been ignoring his calls and texts for weeks."

"That's why he thinks you have a motive."

"Yes, and I guess he's right. I did have a motive."

"A weak one."

"Should I tell the sheriff?"

An excellent question. There were good arguments on both sides.

"I can't tell you that, Daisy. Only you can decide."

It was sort of a copout but I honestly wasn't sure which way I thought she should go.

"There's no one to tell the sheriff. He would probably never find out."

"True."

"But I don't like keeping secrets. They're dangerous. That's what you thought when you came here. You wanted me to tell the sheriff."

"That's true but I didn't know what Colin was talking about then. Now that I do, I think you would be right either way. This is your business, not anyone else's. I can't imagine how Jack would find this out unless Colin had a journal or something and he took the time to write it down."

"I think that I need to think some more."

"Good idea. Don't make any rash decisions. Sleep on it if you like."

My hand reached for the door knob, but I jumped backward when I heard someone on the other side of the door pounding on it. What in the heck? Daisy called for them to come in and Missy flew through the door, her cheeks bright pink and breathing heavy. It looked like she'd run the entire way here from the bookstore.

"Are you okay? What's going on?" I asked, reaching into my purse for the bottle of water I carried around with me. Missy had opened her mouth a few times, but no words had come out. She needed something to drink immediately.

She slugged down half the bottle before answering. "Gavin Baldwin is back in town. He's at the sheriff's station."

Now this was an interesting turn. Just what did that man have to say for himself?

Chapter Thirteen

THE GOSSIP MILL had failed me when it came to finding out Gavin's story, but I consoled myself by working up an appetite for lunch wrestling spreadsheets to the ground and returning a few phone calls. By one o'clock my stomach was growling, and I'd entered approximately one billion invoices into the computer. Okay, it probably wasn't that many, but I wasn't far off. I'd been extraordinarily productive, and I was planning to reward myself with some dessert. Maybe a slice of pie or a slab of chocolate cake.

I stopped by the front desk to check on my newest hire, Tina, who had done a fine job so far. She used to work at the florist shop a few blocks away but had found she was allergic to roses. Needless to say, she'd needed a new job.

"Is everything okay?" I asked her. "Do you need anything?"

"All good," she said with a smile. "Almost everyone that was scheduled to check out today has done so. Only one straggler that needed a late checkout time."

"That's fine. We're not fully booked. If he needs to spend another night, we can accommodate that."

"His situation is sort of up in the air." Tina nodded toward the dining room which was about half full. "He just returned from the sheriff's office. He might be able to tell you his plans."

I wasn't sure who she was talking about. "He?"

"Henry Galbraith."

Henry stayed with us once a month, like clockwork. He had for several years now.

"The salesman?"

Tina laughed and shook her head. "You haven't heard the latest? He's not a salesman. He's a US Marshal. He was watching over Gavin Baldwin."

I glanced over my shoulder at the door of my office. "How long was I in there? No, I clearly haven't heard the latest. What did I miss?"

Tina's eyes lit up. It wasn't often that she had the opportunity to tell me the scoop in Ravenmist.

"Gavin Baldwin is in the witness protection program. He was some bad ass hit man for the mob or something and they need him to testify so they placed him in Ravenmist."

That sounded...far too outrageous to be true.

"Tina, you can't believe everything people tell you—"

"It's true," she interrupted indignantly. "I heard it from Carol, who heard it directly from Selma who works for the sheriff. Gavin Baldwin is in the mafia and Henry Galbraith is the US Marshal that comes to check on him every month and make sure he's following the rules and isn't sleeping with the fishes."

Selma usually did have correct information. She was Jack's

newest administrative assistant and according to him she was so efficient she'd single-handedly replaced three people.

"Gavin Baldwin is in the mafia," I repeated, if only to try out the words for myself. They didn't feel right. "He's a hitman? Are you sure about that part? Because I'd believe he might be the accountant."

"It's always the ones you never suspect," Tina said in a whisper. "The mild-mannered ones turn out to be the serial killers."

I still couldn't picture Gavin as a cold-blooded killer. He had the build and disposition of a teddy bear.

"So what happens now?"

Although I'd asked the question out loud, I didn't expect an answer. It was mostly a query thrown out into the universe. Poor Daisy.

"He'll have to be relocated, of course," Tina answered without missing a beat. "That's why Henry needs a late checkout."

"Does Daisy know?"

Dumb question. If I knew then she knew.

Tina grimaced and then shrugged. "I don't know. Probably. I can't imagine a scenario where she wouldn't."

My appetite forgotten, I turned on my heel and headed back to my office. Just for my coat, though.

"Call me if you need me. I'm going to find Daisy."

She was going to need a friend today.

"I REALLY LOVED you, Daisy. I didn't lie about that. Just about...everything else."

The scene unfolding in front of me was almost too bizarre to be real, but it was actually happening in the interrogation room in the sheriff's station. Although my goal had been Daisy's, I'd passed by the sheriff's station and there she was, standing in the middle of the office and sniffling into a wadded-up tissue. Now we were herded into a more private room along with Gavin, Jack, and the US Marshal Henry Galbraith. Did I mention that he'd told me he was a salesman? There had been quite a few lies floating around our little town it would seem.

"I couldn't tell you the truth," Gavin went on as Daisy cried harder. I patted her shoulder and offered a fresh tissue. "You would have hated me."

Jack rolled his eyes and shifted impatiently on his feet while Henry simply looked on. He didn't appear to be in any hurry to leave. I guess those mobsters weren't a threat at the moment. Thank goodness.

"I wouldn't have hated you, but I almost hate you now," Daisy said in between tears. "You lied to me, Gavin. I deserved better."

"You deserve the best," he replied passionately. "And I want-ed to give that to you. I'm just sorry that I can't."

The couple embraced but it was awkward and clumsy. Gavin didn't want to let go but Daisy obviously did. Eventually Henry stepped forward and clapped a hand on the hitman's shoulder.

"Time to go. We need to get you out of here and to your

next location."

Someone must have been listening at the door because at that precise second it flew open and two uniformed officers were standing on the other side. One on each side of Gavin, they escorted him out of the building with Henry trailing behind. It looked like he'd be checking out of the inn quite soon.

Selma stood from her desk carrying a box of tissues. "Let's get you into the ladies' room, hon. Splash some cold water on your face. No man is worth ruining your mascara over."

The two women scuttled off to the restroom leaving me with Jack. I had questions. Not a lot but a few.

"Was Gavin Baldwin really a hitman for the mob?"

"Yes, and according to Galbraith a particularly vicious one."

"And he was placed here in witness protection?"

"He was."

I looked up at Jack, giving him an accusing stare. "You knew the entire time."

"I did not," he stated in a firm, no-nonsense tone. "Apparently Galbraith had informed the former head lawman but when he retired, he took the secret with him. No one else seemed to know. So I was just as surprised as you were, Tedi."

Oh. That was different and not nearly so awful. I hated to think that Jack knew about Gavin's past but had let Daisy go on and on about him. Then a thought occurred to me and I wanted to smack my forehead because I should have thought of it long before now.

"Then Gavin is the killer."

A heavy sigh. Jack sure did that a bunch when I was around. If he continued, I might take it personally.

"You'd think he'd be the number one subject, but he has an airtight alibi. Galbraith and his minions were watching Baldwin. Turns out they were always watching him, pretty much twenty-four-seven, just in case he got a wild hair and tried to disappear. He and Daisy went to the lake to throw in a rose about eleven-thirty. Then he took her home and took himself home after that."

"They're sure?"

"Very sure. I guess he owes the government testimony in a few more trials. Anyway, they can vouch for him. Gavin Baldwin did not kill Colin Aiken. He killed a few dozen other people, but not Colin."

"Gavin," I murmured, shaking my head. "It defies reason. He was a dairy farmer, for heaven's sake."

"Just a cover story." Jack leaned down so we were almost nose to nose. "Honestly, it's just as well because he would have broken Daisy's heart eventually. He was never meant to stay here forever. Maybe another year or so and then they would have moved him to a new town. He'll be moving around every five years or so for the rest of his life. He ought to be grateful that he isn't rotting in prison because that's exactly where he should be as far as I'm concerned. When I was a cop in Chicago, I hated it when prosecutors cut these kinds of deals and I hate it now. Baldwin did some evil things and he's not going to pay for them."

I couldn't argue because Jack had a point. A really good one. While Gavin's life wasn't going to puppies and rainbows and he'd be looking over his shoulder, it wasn't nearly as awful as it could have been.

"They must have wanted someone even more evil," I finally replied. "But I know that doesn't make it any better. But I agree with you that it's just as well that it happened now before Daisy would be completely and totally heartbroken."

"The world is full of compromise," Jack said, his mouth turned down. "I've had to learn to deal with it, but I can't say that I like it."

I didn't have a chance to reply as Daisy and Selma exited the ladies' room, joining us again in the conference room. Daisy did look better, and she wasn't blowing her nose or dabbing at her eyes any more.

If anything, she looked pretty gosh darn mad. Can't say that I blame her. She'd been dealt a crummy hand these last couple of days. As Gavin had said…she deserved better.

"I'm sorry this all happened this way," Jack said. "If I'd known—"

"You couldn't have told me anyway," Daisy replied, waving away his concern with a shake of her head. "It's alright. This has been a real learning moment for me. I feel wiser than I was this morning."

Wise was good. Right? Except that I hadn't expected Daisy to bounce back so quickly. Surely, she'd want to be sad for a little while longer? Eat some ribs and ice cream. Watch romantic comedies. Or Steven Seagal movies. Whatever made her happy.

"That's wonderful," Selma gushed. "I'm always saying that as bad as any situation is, we can always learn from it and become better people."

Selma *was* always saying that, and it was kind of annoying.

"That's why I'm swearing off men for good." Daisy nodded and then pointed right at me. "I'm going to be just like you, Tedi. All alone with no one else in my life."

Ummm...I was no role model. This might have taken a turn for the worst. What could I do to fix it?

And even more importantly. If Gavin wasn't the killer, then who was?

Chapter Fourteen

THE PLAN WAS to have dinner with Dad and Kate in the dining room at the inn, but I was worried about Daisy and suggested that we eat at The Grateful Raven. The idea was enthusiastically approved and that's how I found myself sitting in a booth across from my dad, Dan Hamilton, and his new girlfriend Kate. He'd ordered the rotisserie chicken dinner and she'd ordered fettucine alfredo, which was the special of the evening. After weighing my options, I'd settled on the turkey dinner. With any luck the tryptophan in the meat would help me fall asleep later.

But until the food arrived, we couldn't simply sit here in awkward silence. I needed to start a friendly conversation. Weather was always good.

"So Kate, Dad tells me that you lived in Florida for several years. It must be quite a change to be in this wintry weather."

If Kate thought my attempt was lame, she was too polite to say so.

"It is quite different but I'm actually enjoying the cold and snow. I really missed the change of seasons when I lived in

Florida. It was lovely to have sunny and warm weather most of the time but believe it or not, it can get monotonous. What about you? Do you like the snow?"

"I love snow, but I admit that I'm kind of a wimp when it comes to the cold."

Dad laughed and sipped at his iced tea. "That's an understatement. Tedi hates the cold and the minute the temperature drops below fifty degrees she's wrapped up in a winter coat, boots, and gloves."

"Don't forget the earmuffs," I said, giving him a wink. "I don't like my ears to get cold, either."

"I completely agree," Kate replied. "The best part of the cold weather is when you get inside and can sit in front of the fire with a nice glass of brandy, all cozy and warm."

"By the beginning of March, I'm ready for a tropical beach and lots of sunshine."

"I didn't live near the beach but I can recommend a few," Kate offered. "Running the horse farm was a lot of work but we did try and get away from it all every now and then."

My dad placed his arm around Kate's shoulders. "Tedi has always loved horses, haven't you, pumpkin?"

I had but more in the abstract. As in they were beautiful but big. Kind of intimidating.

"I think they're gorgeous but I'm not much of a rider," I confessed. "I've only been a few times and they're so much larger than I am they scare me a little."

"We should all go riding when the weather is better. I'd be

happy to give you some pointers," Kate offered warmly. She truly seemed like a nice person, and it wouldn't be a hardship spending time with her. "Choosing the correct mount is important."

The two times I'd been riding I was sure they'd given me horses that hadn't broken into a trot in over a decade. Mostly they'd just wanted to wander around and eat grass.

"That's a wonderful idea," Dad agreed. "There's a place to rent horses not far from here. Tedi, you could invite the sheriff and his son to go with us."

"Why?"

The question was out before I could stop it. But it was still an excellent question.

Frowning, Kate's gaze darted back and forth between me and my dad. "I thought you and the sheriff... I saw you two having lunch the other day..."

"No," I replied firmly. "Not at all. We're just friends."

Even if we were a couple, I simply couldn't picture Jack sitting on a horse of his own free will. He had city boy written all over him. Now Tyler was a different story. He'd probably love it. I could imagine inviting him.

"You could do worse, pumpkin."

"So I've been told. The town consensus seems to be that I couldn't do any better."

Kate elbowed Dan. "I'm sure you could. You're beautiful and successful. Any man would be lucky to date you."

She was becoming my favorite person in Ravenmist.

"I'm not sure about any man but thank you, Kate. I'm just not looking to find anyone right now." Which brought me to the subject of Daisy and what had happened this afternoon. "I'm not sure you heard but apparently my single status is now the envy of Daisy. She's sworn off men because she wants to be just like me. Alone."

I admit it. Her words still stung a little bit. I wasn't alone. I had friends, family...even ghosts that I spent time with. Daisy had made me sound like a recluse in a tower.

Dad glanced around the restaurant. "I did hear actually, so when you asked to eat here, I understood why. Where is she? I haven't seen her all evening."

He wouldn't have from his vantage point, but Daisy had been hovering around the kitchen entrance since we'd arrived. She'd stick her head out for a minute or two and then disappear again. It looked like she was watching for someone.

"She's here," I answered. "But keeping to the kitchen. Can't say that I blame her with everything that's gone on. I'd want to keep a low profile."

Kate nodded in agreement. "That's wise. Just keep her head down until this all blows over. I'm told she's a major suspect."

That last part was said in a soft whisper.

It was true. Daisy was still a suspect since the US Marshals hadn't been watching her at the time of the murder, only Gavin. And Jack wasn't going to let this fade away. He'd keep at it like a dog with a bone until he found the killer. And if it wasn't Gavin, then the suspicion was going to swing back to Daisy and Jane.

Add in that Colin had pointed the finger at Daisy and this entire situation didn't look good. At all. Luckily Jack had no idea that the victim had named Daisy as the guilty party.

"I hope Garrett finds the murderer soon," my dad said as our dinner plates were slid in front of us. "Then this town can go back to normal. Everybody's jumpy right now with the thought of a killer on the loose."

Kate placed her napkin in her lap and then picked up her fork. "I doubt they have anything to fear. From what I've heard around town Colin Aiken was murdered because he'd done bad things to good people. Isn't that why Daisy is a suspect? It was a love gone wrong thing?"

"There is no way that Daisy did this."

My tone was rather more harsh than I'd intended but I didn't like people gossiping about a friend who was completely innocent.

Kate's brows went up. "I meant no disrespect, Tedi. I was only saying that there doesn't seem to be any other suspects now."

"There are others," I replied immediately. "Colin Aiken had at least one other girlfriend that he was cheating on and we don't know how many more. There are plenty of people that might have wanted him dead."

"Honey," my dad said gently. "Of course we don't think Daisy is guilty."

"And even if she was," Kate added. "It sounds like this Colin Aiken deserved it. He wasn't a good person."

That was one way to put it, although being a crappy person usually didn't come with the death penalty. I'd always assumed that karmic reincarnation would take effect and they'd come back in their next life as a worm.

"He did have…issues," I said with a grimace. "But it was a terrible way to go out. Kind of grisly."

My father's expression turned somber. "I think I'd like to go out in my sleep like my own dad. He laid down to take a nap one day after lunch. It was his favorite, too. Shepherd's pie. Mom made a good one."

"That's much better than how my late husband passed on," Kate said with a sad smile. "He was under a great deal of stress and had a heart attack. He was far too young. We had so many plans."

Dad reached over and squeezed Kate's hand. "I'm sorry that you had to deal with that."

"It wasn't easy." Kate's voice had dropped to almost a whisper. "The final arrangements. The horse farm. Lawyers and real estate agents. It seemed like every time I turned around there was another problem. Jim had handled most of the business side while I dealt with the horses, so I didn't have a clue how to even log onto our bank account. I had to learn it all. The hard way."

I did feel badly for Kate. From the sound of it, she'd had a raw deal all around. No wonder she'd moved home so she could be closer to family.

"We're glad you're here in Ravenmist," I said and meant it. "Hopefully it will be much smoother from here on out."

Kate smiled at Dad. "It already is."

It looked like they might be in love. I hadn't been the biggest fan of their relationship, but it might not be the worst thing in the world. My dad was happy and that meant so much to me. He deserved it. From now on I'd be his biggest cheerleader.

DAD WAS PAYING the check – I'd tried to give him my share, but he wouldn't take it – when Missy waltzed into the restaurant. I hadn't spoken to her most of the day, but I was glad to see her. She was dressed in her warmest clothes and I couldn't help but wonder if she'd been out to the lake to see the Young Lovers.

"Hey, I didn't expect to see you here."

Missy glanced at my dad and Kate before giving me a strange look, her eyes wide and her brows lifted comically high. Okay, something was definitely going on. As usual, I was the last to hear about it.

"I came over to see Daisy."

"She's in the kitchen."

"I know." Missy paused. "You should come with me to talk to her."

Before I could answer, Dad stood and helped Kate to her feet. "That sounds like a good idea, pumpkin. Daisy could use some good friends right about now. Please let her know that we're thinking about her and if she needs anything…well…just let us know."

"I will." Dad enfolded me in a bear hug so big it lifted me off my feet. Kate smiled, and we hugged too, albeit much less personal. More of a hug-lite, but it was I hoped the beginning of a friendship. If she was going to be in Dad's life, I wanted us to be on the best of terms. "I'm glad we could get together. We should do this every week. Next time I pick up the check."

Dad shrugged into his coat. "You'll need to be faster off the mark then, but that sounds like a great idea. I'll text you and we can set something up."

"I'm looking forward to that," Kate said. "Maybe we can try the new steakhouse on the edge of town."

I'd heard good things but hadn't been there yet.

"I'm in. I love a good steak and potato."

Dad dropped a kiss on my forehead. "We'll call you. Stay warm out there."

Rolling my eyes, I groaned. "I will. It's not that bad outside. Just a normal February night."

Dad and Kate left leaving me with Missy, who placed her hand on my shoulder and leaned in close so no one could overhear.

"I'm glad you don't think it's too cold outside because that's exactly where we're going."

"Outside? Why?"

Was this some weird female bonding ritual? Couldn't we just buy shoes instead? Preferably in a nice warm mall with a food court.

"Daisy called me. She wants the three of us to go out to the lake so she can get her rose back. She doesn't want to be in love with Gavin for the rest of her life."

I wasn't following the logic. If there was any.

"She threw the rose in the lake. It's gone. How can she get it back?"

Missy rubbed her chin and grinned. "Magic."

Say what?

"You're joking."

"I'm not. Daisy did a search on the internet and found an un-love spell. We're going to the lake to cast it, so you'll need to put on your winter woolens."

"She found it on the internet?" I echoed. "Well, of course it will work then. Why didn't I think of that?"

Yes, there was sarcasm in my tone. I'm sorry but I couldn't help it. A spell?

"Daisy believes it will work so we're going to do it," Missy said firmly. "It could work. We don't know."

"Are witches and magic real?"

"I have no idea, but I think we're about to find out."

The bell over the door rang again and in walked my mother. She was also dressed as if she was going on an expedition to the North Pole. Wait...my mother?

"Mom?"

"Tedi."

"Why are you here?"

"The same reason you are, I would expect. You're going to freeze in that coat."

"I didn't know I was going anywhere until a few minutes ago. Why are you going?"

Peggy Hamilton beamed with happiness. "Because I'm going to help."

My life is so bizarre. Someone hold me.

"Help? How so?"

"I ran into Daisy this afternoon. When she told me what she was going to do I offered to come help. The spell says that more people give off more energy. I want to do my part."

I was off to cast a spell with my friend, my mother, and the Grim Reaper. Nothing to see here, folks. Just another day in Ravenmist.

Chapter Fifteen

"**I** HAVE TERRIBLE taste in men."

Daisy's declaration cut through the silence as the four of us stood on the banks of the lake. My mother was holding a piece of paper that contained the spell and looking at it with a small flashlight.

"We all make mistakes," my mother said in a soothing tone. "You couldn't have known about Gilbert."

"Gavin," I whispered, nudging my mom's arm. "His name is Gavin. Or at least I think it is. The government probably gave him a new name. I don't know what his real one is."

"You couldn't have known about Gavin," Peggy repeated, this time a little louder. "He's an excellent liar."

"I should have known about Colin," Daisy said. "Everybody else knew."

Well…yes. But love was blind and all of those old sayings.

"You have a full and open heart," Missy said. "That's a blessing and a curse. It means you can get hurt easily but it also means that you can find love again."

Daisy snorted. "I don't want to love again, and I certainly

don't want to love Gavin for the rest of my life. I want my rose back."

"Eventually you'll want to fall in love again," Peggy replied. "That's what I tell Tedi."

That was the truth. My mother had said it several times but so far, she was wrong.

But Daisy was a different story. I wanted her to be happy and I knew deep down that she wanted to be in love. Right now, she was hurt and scared but in the future she wouldn't want to be alone.

You know…like me.

I was happy alone. Right now. But maybe someday I might want to share my life with someone. It could happen.

"I just want to get my rose back and fall out of love with Gavin."

Daisy wanted instant gratification. She wanted to miss all the pain of a breakup and finding out that the man she loved was a big liar and jerk. Since there wasn't a regular way of going about that we were here to see if magic would work. I wasn't optimistic.

So let's get to it because it was darn cold out here.

"What do we do first?" I asked, hoping to move this train along the tracks. "What does the spell say?"

Mom tapped the paper with the flashlight.

"This is an un-love spell. It says to take all of the personal items that remind you of your beloved and to place them in an earthenware pot and set them on fire. As the flames turn them to ash, we need to send out positive energy into the universe."

"That's it? My roommate did that in college except she used a Winnie the Pooh trash can."

Although it was iffy about the positive energy. She'd been pretty mad that night.

"Did it work?" Missy asked.

"It seemed to. She started dating another guy a few weeks later. Seriously though, that's all it says? Don't we need an eye of newt or some bat wings? Isn't there an incantation we need to chant?"

What kind of discount witchcraft was this, anyway?

"You've watched too many movies," Peggy said bluntly. "The best spells are the simplest."

"You're a witch now?"

"I bet that's one of the nicer things you and your sisters called me when you were teenagers," my mother laughed. "But no, I'm not a witch. I looked it up on the internet."

Then it had to be true.

"Besides, we don't have any bat wings," Missy explained patiently. "Or any way to get them. I, for one, am glad that we only have to have positive thoughts. Is that going to be an issue for you? Because we can't have any Negative Nellies here tonight. It will ruin the spell."

Everyone was an expert on spells all of a sudden. Did the entire town think I was a drag to be around?

"I am not a Negative Nellie," I protested hotly to no one in particular. My voice sounded loud out here. Too loud. I sounded defensive as well. "I'm perfectly happy."

"Of course, you are," Peggy said in that tone again, as if I was a small child. "We just need to make sure."

"Well, I'm happy."

Except now I didn't sound it. Honestly, I was a little perturbed. I was beginning to think that there were people in my life that had a skewed idea of my emotional maturity. I wasn't bitter, I was cautious. Right?

"So do you have all of your mementos?" Missy asked. "We can put them here in this planter."

It was the closest thing to an *earthenware pot* that we had. A nice terracotta planter that we'd snatched from the barn at the inn. There'd been a whole stack of them and we'd chosen the largest one we could carry.

"I do. It's mostly ticket stubs and a few takeout menus. I already deleted the photos from my phone. There is a silk scarf he bought for me."

The scarf was multi-colored and quite pretty, but the way Daisy shoved it in the bottom of the planter it might have been two-week-old bananas, shriveled and black. The paper items were placed on top and my mother pulled a lighter out of her coat pocket.

"We banish these memories into the universe," Peggy intoned, her gaze resting on the lake where the rose had been thrown. "Daisy no longer wants to love Gavin. So begone with this emotional tether."

Not bad. My mom might have made a decent witch if she'd

wanted to go that way. It sounded very official and that was the important part. This was for Daisy and to help her move on.

"Begone," Missy repeated.

"Begone," I repeated as well, getting into the spirit of the occasion.

"Begone," Daisy echoed, raising her arms to shoulder height and waving her hands toward the water. "Begone, Gavin. Bring on the new."

Mom lit the corner of a paper in the planter and it only took a moment for the fire to grow. We all stared out onto the lake and I closed my eyes, trying to think of the most positive thoughts I could. Apple pie, chocolate ice cream, warm sunshine, comfortable beds, and good books. I threw in cuddly puppies and cocoa for good measure. No one could stay grumpy while holding a puppy and drinking cocoa. It wasn't physically possible.

"I want my love to begone, too."

My eyes snapped open at the sound of that voice. I recognized it, of course.

Amelia.

This was about to get...weird. And for Ravenmist, that was saying something.

STOMPING AND THROWING his hands up in the air, Charles was right behind Amelia.

"I can't believe you're doing this. You really want me to be gone?"

Amelia rounded on him so they were almost eye to eye. "I don't want to be in love with you anymore. We're always arguing, Charles, and I'm tired of it."

After more than a hundred years it had to get on the nerves. Fighting about the same subjects over and over.

Charles seemed at a loss for words, shaking his head and pacing back and forth, but eventually he did speak. "But...we love each other."

"It doesn't feel that way to me. Does it to you?"

It felt like we shouldn't be watching this. It was far too personal and painful, and I wondered if we all should cover our ears or something so they could have some privacy. Then I remembered that Daisy and Mom were probably almost peeing their pants at seeing two ghosts work out their relationship issues right in front of their eyes.

One look at my mother told the tale. Her eyes were round and her mouth hung open in surprise. Daisy had the identical expression on her face. Whatever they'd been thinking the evening would be it had taken a turn for the bizarre and supernatural.

"If you don't love me anymore there's no point in hanging around here," Charles said, his lips pressed together. "I might as well move on and into the light."

Just as he finished saying the word a beam of light shone down just as it had with Colin Aiken. Missy morphed into her

Grim Reaper persona, drawing gasps from Daisy and my mom, who had to be wondering if they'd hit their heads at some point tonight.

"Oops!" Missy whispered. "I can't control it when they call out to the light. I guess we're going to have to explain this."

I guess we were, but I didn't even know where to begin.

Hey Mom, did I mention that my best friend was a Reaper? Oh, and there's a ghost that lives in my closet. No, I haven't been drinking. Why do you ask?

Amelia stepped between Charles and the beam of light. "You'd just leave me? Leave me out here alone?"

"If you don't believe I love you then what's the point of staying? I've devoted my whole life to you, Amelia-mine." His tone was passionate and earnest. "I love you more than anyone else in the world."

Amelia launched herself at her centuries-old lover and they kissed, murmuring words that I was sorely glad that we couldn't hear. They'd reconciled, and it was kind of romantic in a squishy sort of way. The light disappeared as quickly as it had come, and Missy turned blurry before morphing back into her everyday, normal self.

We still had a whole lot to explain, though.

Missy cleared her throat. "I suppose you're wondering what's going on here?"

I almost raised my hand and asked her to explain it to me.

My mother was the first to speak. She was rarely at a loss for words. "I have questions and you two are going to answer them."

Daisy nodded, her gaze still on the embracing couple. "I have questions as well."

I glanced at Missy and shrugged my shoulders. We were well down the rabbit hole so I was just going to go with it.

"Missy is the Grim Reaper," I stated loudly. "If that answers one of your questions. She escorts dead souls to the afterlife."

Daisy blinked a few times and shook her head. "Believe it or not, that wasn't my question."

"Then you probably want to know about Amelia and Charles," Missy said, her tone rushed. "They're...spirits from the past that didn't cross over."

"They're the Young Lovers," my mom breathed, her eyes still round. "They're real. It's not just a story."

"They're real," I agreed, moving to my mother's side and placing an arm around her shoulders. "Ghosts are real."

I couldn't keep the glee out of my voice. I was still that excited about it.

"I always assumed they were, but I guess I never thought I would be lucky enough to see one," Peggy replied. "I've heard this story every year for my entire life and now here they are. The Young Lovers. In the flesh."

"Um, Mom...they're not exactly in the flesh."

Peggy gave me a blinding smile. "Close enough. This is so exciting. They're real. They're really real."

The couple seemed to notice that they were the topic of conversation and broke away from one another to stare at the four people staring at them.

Missy, bless her, tried to smooth over the situation. "Amelia. Charles. This is Daisy and Peggy. They're our friends."

The Young Lovers eyed them up and down and seemed to decide that they were harmless. Charles placed his arm around Amelia's waist.

"I don't want to move on anymore. You can't make me."

"No, I can't, and I won't," Missy assured him. "We just want you to be happy."

"How can you be happy out here?" Daisy queried. She'd finally found her voice. "It's lonely and desolate here. Not to mention all the people that come out here on Valentine's Day. You need to be somewhere homier. With people you can talk to. That's probably why you argue. You only have each other."

Amelia gazed cautiously at her beloved. "It might be nice to have someone else to talk to on occasion."

"I don't want to argue," Charles said. "I want us to be happy. Like we used to be."

"I bet you had lots of friends then," Daisy said. "Not just each other."

Charles nodded in, his lips turned down sadly. "We did but they're all gone now."

"That doesn't mean you have to be all alone," my mother said. "There are people all over town."

Daisy and Mom still had no idea that there were ghosts all over Ravenmist, either. That they might have even interacted with a few at the ball the other night.

"I have a lovely attic above the restaurant," Daisy said, her hands clasped together in delight. "Lots of space and very clean, with plenty of people in and out daily. You can come and live with me."

Hold the phone. Did Daisy just offer the Young Lovers a home? It would appear that she did.

AMELIA AND CHARLES sat in the back-row seats of my mother's minivan – not that they needed a conveyance to move around. After surprisingly little discussion, they'd accepted Daisy's offer of the attic over The Grateful Raven. Now we were all headed to their new home.

This was complete and totally surreal.

In the space of only a few minutes Daisy had adopted two ghosts who were over a hundred years old. I was still in shock. Amelia and Charles had shown absolutely no interest in other people, ghosts, or leaving the lake in a century and now suddenly they were going to live in town.

All because Amelia had wanted to get rid of her love for Charles and he'd threatened to go into the light.

And did I mention poor Missy? She'd lost out on another soul.

She leaned closer to me, whispering in my ear. "The spell worked."

Mom had the radio on so no one could hear our conversation. "What do you mean *it worked*? How did it work?"

Missy nodded toward a smiling Daisy riding shotgun. "She's happy. She hasn't even thought about Gavin Baldwin since she met the Young Lovers, and she won't be alone anymore. It worked."

All be darned...it had worked. Not in the way that I'd assumed it would, but Daisy wasn't crying, sad, and lonely.

"We still have a problem, though."

I hated to be the bearer of bad news, but this wasn't quite the perfect happy ending.

"What problem?"

"Daisy is still a suspect in Colin Aiken's murder now that Gavin is out of the picture."

"Oh. Right."

"We have to do something about that."

"What can we do?"

I didn't know yet, but I wouldn't give up. Someone had murdered Colin and it wasn't Daisy. Eventually they'd trip up and reveal themselves. I only hoped it would be sooner rather than later.

Chapter Sixteen

I T WAS JUST after breakfast the next day and I'd had two cups of coffee when a stunning middle-aged woman entered the front door of the inn, rolling a medium-sized suitcase behind her and a laptop bag over her arm. She was tall and willowy, with dark hair and the most vivid blue eyes I think I'd ever seen in my life. She had an air of wealth about her, from the red soles of her Louboutin high heels to the Louis Vuitton leather handbag slung over one arm.

Innkeeper instinct kicked in hard and I immediately went to relieve her of her burden, which she graciously gave up with a murmured thank you. On closer inspection she looked tired as if she might have been traveling all night. There were dark circles under her eyes and her shoulders drooped slightly despite not carrying a bag to drag them down.

"Hello and welcome to the Ravenmist Inn," I said. "Are you looking for a room?"

"I am and I'm hoping you have one. I could use a hot meal and some solid sack time."

"We can do both of those," I assured her. "Let's quickly get you checked in."

Sharon the desk manager was on a break, so I sat down behind the desk, fingers poised on the keyboard.

"How long are you planning to stay?"

"I'm not sure. Is that a problem?"

"Not at all. We've entered the slow season." I pulled up the perfect room with a view overlooking the expansive backyard. "Is it just you in your party?"

"Yes."

"Name?"

"Doctor Elisabetta Aiken."

My fingertips had automatically typed in the name before my brain caught up. "Aiken?"

"A-i-k-e-n," she spelled out loud. "Aiken."

Jack had said that Colin's wife was a doctor in Miami. This woman did have something of a tan…in February.

"Got it. Now your address?"

The doctor reeled off a Miami address and I knew for sure. This was Colin Aiken's estranged wife. Why was she here?

The rest of the check-in process went smoothly although Doctor Aiken appeared even more tired by the end of it. I had a million questions I wanted to ask her but were basically none of my business, so I kept my lips sealed. It wasn't easy, though. It was almost a relief when I handed her luggage off to Kevin who escorted her up to her room.

I reached for my cell in my blazer pocket. Did Jack know she was in town?

"I don't have time for this, Tedi," he barked into the phone when he picked up. "I'm busy here."

"Well, I'm busy here, too," I retorted. "But I thought you should know that Doctor Elisabetta Aiken is here. She just checked in and went up to sleep. Did you know she was coming?"

There was silence and then I could hear him take a breath.

"Yes, but I didn't know when."

"Is she here to talk to you? Help you find the killer?"

"I've already found the killer, Tedi. That's what I've been trying to tell you."

"You found the killer?" I echoed, dumbfounded. Of all the words I expected him to say, those weren't it.

"I did. I arrested Jane Allerton this morning."

Oh my.

I WASN'T PROUD of it, but I lured Jack over to the inn with a promise of a hot meal. It worked. He was now sitting in my kitchen wolfing down an open-faced turkey sandwich with gravy and mashed potatoes. I could practically hear his arteries screaming for mercy. They weren't going to get any because he was already eyeing some apple pie for dessert.

A la mode.

He shoved a forkful into his mouth and chewed blissfully. The sandwich was the lunch special today.

"I know you didn't invite me over here out of the goodness of your heart. So spit it out. What do you want?"

He wasn't nearly as smart as he thought he was if he didn't already know.

"The details, of course. So spit it out," I mocked.

"They'll be in tonight's paper. I gave the full story to Gus."

Gus was the crime reporter in Ravenmist. In addition, he covered all the other sections in the newspaper including the movie reviews and wedding announcements. He was also the advice columnist and had been known to start a few town wars a time or two over his answers.

"And you're sitting here now. C'mon, you know you want to tell me or else you wouldn't have accepted my invitation."

"You say that every time."

"And you fall for it. So talk."

Jack wiped his mouth with the paper napkin. "Fine, Jane Allerton's alibi fell apart. A traffic camera caught her driving back into town. When I questioned her about it, she admitted that she was coming back into town to talk to Colin, but she swears she didn't kill him."

"I doubt that's enough to arrest her."

"It isn't."

"So?"

"The rest is going to cost you a slice of pie and a scoop of vanilla ice cream."

"I don't know how you keep your girlish figure, Sheriff, but keep talking while I cut you a piece of pie. Do you want whipped cream?"

"I'll pass. I really should watch what I eat."

"You seem to watch it as it goes from your fork to your mouth." I slid a large slice of pie onto a plate and carried it over to the freezer for the ice cream. "So what else did you find?"

"Forensics found voicemails from Jane to Colin on his phone where she threatened him with bodily harm and yes, even death. We have a recording of her saying that he deserved to die. She knew he was cheating on her and had for weeks."

Making a sour face, I placed the plate in front of Jack along with a fresh fork. I had a weird thing about people reusing their forks. I know, it's strange but that's me.

"I don't think I'd make a big deal about a guy cheating on me if I hadn't been dating him all that long. I'd dump him and move on with my life."

"The phone messages went back four months. They were dating longer than she'd said. She lied about that, too."

"Can you arrest someone for making violent threats?"

"You can if their fingerprints are on the murder weapon."

"Ah, I guess that would be what my dad would call a major indicator."

"To be fair, your fingerprints are on the bow and arrow too, as are many others. Lots of guests touched it but then they didn't have a reason to want Aiken dead."

"That we know of," I replied automatically. "I know I'm just a civilian but that doesn't seem like much evidence. It sounds...circumstantial."

I'd heard the word a ton of times on "Law and Order".

"I can't count the number of people that have been found guilty on less. She had motive, means, and opportunity. Plus, forensics ties her to the murder weapon."

"But she still denies it."

"Loudly, but she's lawyering up so I'm guessing he will tell her to stop talking. They always do. It's not like she's sitting in a cell rotting away to nothing. She's already made bail and called me every name in the book."

"Did she hurt your feelings?"

He scraped the last bit of apple pie from the plate with his fork. "My feelings aren't that delicate, thank goodness. I don't blame her for hating me. I don't take it personally. She's upset because she got arrested. She got arrested because I'd be a lousy cop if I didn't bring her in."

"She may not have killed Aiken."

Somehow, I couldn't picture Jane Allerton shooting that arrow into Colin Aiken's heart.

"That's true, but at the very least she's a liar, and she should know not to lie during a murder investigation. It makes you look guilty."

Jack made a decent argument but...

"I simply can't picture Jane Allerton as a killer. I just don't get that vibe from her."

"That's what they said about Ted Bundy."

"Are you comparing Jane to Ted Bundy? That's quite a leap."

"No, but who really knows what others are capable of? Some people might look mild and meek but when pushed they could kill."

"Could you kill?"

I don't know why I asked the question. He was a cop, so of course his answer would be yes. Our gazes collided, and he leaned down so were almost nose to nose.

"Yes, and I bet you could too, if you had to."

"I think you don't know me very well."

"I think you don't know yourself."

"I'm still not sure about Jane Allerton."

"If you've got a better suspect, I'm listening."

I didn't. Despite Colin Aiken's declarations, I knew good and well that Daisy was innocent.

"Are you absolutely sure Gavin Baldwin isn't the killer?"

Okay, I was grasping at straws.

"The marshal vouched for him, Tedi. He didn't do it. It would be convenient but unfortunately that's not going to happen."

I threw up my hands in frustration. "What about all the other people that Colin has pissed off? There have to be a myriad of suspects."

Jack nodded. "There are dozens of people that wouldn't mind seeing Aiken dead. The problem is they either were miles away or their fingerprints weren't on the murder weapon."

"They could have worn gloves," I shot back. "That doesn't mean anything."

"Aiken hasn't lived in Illinois all that long," Jack said with a sigh. "Before that he was in Florida and yes, there are plenty of suspects there, but they all check out. They weren't anywhere in the vicinity when he was killed. I keep coming back to Jane Allerton."

"Means, motive, and opportunity," I murmured, feeling deflated. He'd countered all of my arguments. "I just can't see it, though."

"That's because you would never commit murder over a man. But there are people who will, Tedi."

I wanted to reply that they didn't do that in Ravenmist but clearly, they did because we had a murder to solve.

"So what are you going to do about Colin Aiken's wife?"

Standing, Jack checked his phone briefly and then slid it in his pocket. "Give her the good news that we've made an arrest. Offer her my condolences. When she wakes up and comes downstairs will you give me a call? I'll come here to meet her. She doesn't need to come to the station."

"I will," I promised. "I guess I should congratulate you on closing this case. That's two for two."

"Just doing my job."

He said it so modestly I couldn't help but laugh. Jack wasn't a humble kind of guy.

"You sound like those guys on television after their team wins. *I was just being a team player. I just want the team to do well.*"

He grinned and shrugged into his coat. "That's me. The

ultimate team player. Thanks for lunch and the pie."

"If you don't eat a vegetable, Jack, you're going to die young."

"But what a life I will have lived."

No regrets. I envied him.

Chapter Seventeen

I'D DISAPPEARED INTO my office after lunch but was dragged out around three by one of my waitstaff when Doctor Aiken came downstairs to the dining room. She was seated at a two-top near the windows, sipping coffee and nibbling at a Cobb salad. She'd changed her clothes and was dressed more casually in jeans, sweater, and boots.

I'd already sent a text to Jack that the doctor was awake, but I felt compelled to offer my own condolences to the widow. They may have been living separate lives at the end, but they were still married and at one point had probably been happy.

I approached her cautiously, not wanting to disturb her meal. If she scowled, I'd hightail it out of her space.

"Doctor Aiken, I hope you had a good rest. Is there anything I can get for you? Please just let us know if there's anything we can do."

The woman shook her head and took a sip of her coffee. "I'm fine. The bed was very comfortable, and I was able to get some sleep, thank you." She paused for a moment before continuing. "I suppose you know why I'm here."

"It's a small town," I replied ruefully. "There aren't many secrets in Ravenmist, Doctor Aiken."

"I suppose not," she said with a wan smile. "Would you care to join me? It's Tedi, right? It's lonely eating by myself."

"It is Tedi. I will join you but let me first get you a refill on your coffee."

I retrieved the carafe from the warmer in the corner of the dining room, refilled her cup, filled one for myself, and then settled into the other chair.

Where was Jack? The station wasn't that far from the inn. I would have thought he'd be here within minutes.

"Is there anything else I can get you, Doctor? Anything at all?"

She shook her head. "No, thank you. This salad is lovely, though."

Small talk. As an innkeeper I was used to it. But like a bartender I was also used to hearing personal details from people I'd never met before and would never see again. I was sure that was my allure...a total stranger to tell your troubles to. I was getting the distinct feeling that Doctor Elisabetta Aiken wanted to talk to someone but didn't have anyone to actually talk to.

"The dinner special tonight is Chicken Piccata. I highly recommend it."

"I'll give it a try." She placed her fork on the edge of her plate. "Did you know my husband?"

Straight and to the point. Here we go.

"Not really. I'd seen him around town and he...dated a

friend of mine."

"It's okay. We had an understanding."

I didn't know what to say. I'd never met a couple with an understanding.

"That's good, then."

Was it? At this point I didn't know, and I didn't want to make her feel worse than she already did.

Doctor Aiken dabbed at the corners of her mouth with the snowy white napkin. "My relationship with Colin was complicated. We were both young when we met, and he swept me off of my feet. I came from a formal, stiff family that didn't show much emotion. Colin was the polar opposite and when I was with him, I felt so decadent and free. We married quickly, and it was okay for awhile and then it wasn't. By the time I finished med school I regretted marry him."

Once again, I wasn't sure what to say but she clearly needed a sympathetic ear. I wondered if she had many friends, considering she'd come to Ravenmist all alone.

"I know what Colin was like. I'm not a stupid woman. I can say that he was different when he was younger," she said, a faraway look in her eyes. "Charming and funny. So romantic. He encouraged me to wear bright colors and grow my hair long. He liked to go dancing and we laughed all of the time. He called me Bitty and even named his little boat the same. He'd bring flowers for no reason and he was incredibly spontaneous. He'd wake me up in the middle of the night to drive us to the beach for the sunrise. I loved that about him. I'm rather rigid and conventional in my regular life."

Now that I had a closer view of her, I could see the merest traces of tears on the doctor's face. She'd been crying at some point. My heart squeezed tightly in sympathy.

"I'm so sorry for your loss, Doctor."

I really and truly was. Whatever issues Colin Aiken had he didn't deserve to be killed for them.

"Thank you," she replied with a small smile. "I hope he's at peace now. He was a man that was never satisfied with what life gave him. He was always looking for…something."

"If there's anything I can do, please let me know, Doctor."

"I will, thank you. And please call me Liz. Only my patients call me Doctor." She took another sip of her coffee. "Once I wrap up Colin's business here in Illinois I'll be heading back to Miami. He hated it there. Too many people, he said."

"Is that where you and Colin met?"

I must have brought up a happy memory because Liz smiled. "No, we actually met in Orlando at a college party. I lived there during school and spent the rest of the time with my parents in Ocala until I was accepted into a residency in Miami. Colin stayed in Ocala for quite awhile and we commuted back and forth for several years to see one another. He said he didn't like big cities. I think that's how he ended up in this area."

Ocala? That sounded familiar.

"Would you believe that you're the second person that I've met this week that lived in Ocala?"

That had to be weird, right? Just how large a city was it?

"Hmmm, that is funny. Ocala isn't a small town, though. I'd call it mid-sized. It's not one of those places where everyone knows everyone else. There's around sixty thousand people there."

Not exactly Mayberry. It was a coincidence, that's all.

I didn't get a chance to ponder it though, because Jack had just strode into my dining room and was making a beeline for our table.

And he looked none too happy. So what else was new?

WHAT WERE THE odds?

I wasn't a mathematician. I couldn't do long division with-out a calculator, but it seemed strange to me that I'd met two people in the space of a week from the same town in Florida. The town that our murder victim had lived in for a long time.

Could Kate have known Colin before she moved back to Ravenmist? And if she did, what did that mean exactly? Was it all some giant coincidence? Kate hadn't mentioned that she knew Colin Aiken. Had she mentioned it to my dad?

I was sitting in my office contemplating the universe when Jack joined me, throwing himself down into a chair with a heavy groan. He looked like he'd been run through the wringer and it had only been about three and a half hours since I'd last seen him.

"You look terrible."

I thought about softening the blow, but he wasn't that kind of man. He'd prefer me to be blunt because that's how he would be right back.

"I've had a rough afternoon."

"Any particular reason?"

"Mel Pinkerman and his wife Estelle had a small domestic falling out."

I was surprised and yet not shocked. Mel and Estelle were in their sixties and had spent the last forty years arguing. About what the town was never sure, but they seemed to take it seriously. They always reunited though, and things would quiet down for a few months.

"What happened?"

"He told Estelle that she couldn't cook worth a darn, so she threw all his clothes out on the front lawn. The neighbors called me as Mel was trying to gather them up and throw them in the bed of his pickup truck."

This wasn't the first time Estelle had done that. Mel would probably spend the next few days surfing his brother's sofa.

"And you were the lucky one that got to mediate their argument?"

"It was like talking to two people who spoke a foreign language. I had fights with my ex but never like theirs. Have they ever thought about divorce?"

This was the very first time Jack had mentioned his wife.

"I remember when I was a kid someone suggested it to Mel and he looked at them like they had two heads. So I'm going to say that no, they've never considered it."

"Maybe they deserve each other. They'd drive anyone else insane."

"So you had a rough day?"

"I did."

"And I'm guessing you want pie?"

"I wouldn't turn it down."

Did I dare bring it up? Would Jack laugh in my face? Oh well, it wouldn't be the first time.

"Jack, who else's fingerprints were on the bow and arrow?"

He gave me a shrewd look. "I thought you were of the opinion that the killer wore gloves?"

"Humor me," I sighed. "Who else?"

Pulling out his phone, he scrolled to a list and reeled off about a dozen names. Kate's was one of them. But not my dad.

"What's going on in that scary brain of yours, Tedi? I can practically see the wheels turning."

They were turning. The question was whether they were turning clockwise or counter clockwise.

"Did you talk to Doctor Aiken?"

He nodded. "I did. Gave her my condolences. She thanked me and said she'd be around for awhile dealing with Aiken's home and belongings. She seems like a nice woman."

We were both thinking that she was too nice for Aiken but neither of us wanted to speak ill of the dead. From what she'd said, he'd had his good qualities.

"I talked with her a bit while she ate lunch. Did you know

that she and Aiken lived in Ocala for awhile?"

"I remember seeing that in the background information. He had some business dealings there, but he traveled around a lot."

I took a deep breath and gathered my courage. "Kate Beckswith is from Ocala, too."

Jack really was too smart for his own good.

"What are you suggesting here? Do you know something I don't?"

"No," I admitted. "Not really. Kate told me that she was from Ocala and only a few days later I find out that Aiken lived there. Do you think there's a chance that she knew him before?"

"Even if she did, that doesn't mean she's a suspect," he pointed out, always the logical one. "Did she say anything to you?"

"She didn't but I just think it's a funny coincidence."

"If you met two people from New York City in the same week would you think it was strange?"

"No, but New York City has over eight million people and Ocala has about sixty thousand, according to Doctor Aiken. Those are far different odds."

Jack pinched his bottom lip, ruminating on my words. "True. It could just be a crazy coincidence."

"You hate coincidences."

"I do," he conceded. "Because they generally aren't all that innocent. At least, in my experience."

"Then you agree that it's weird?"

"I do." He sat back and sighed heavily. "Are you sure about

this, Tedi? You're suggesting that I check out your father's new girlfriend. He's your father."

I'd been trying not to think about that, frankly. I'd do better at that if Jack didn't bring it up. He wasn't helping.

"All the more reason," I finally replied. "I hope that I'm wrong. He doesn't have to know that you're checking into her background, does he?"

"I'm not planning to tell him."

The way Jack said it he thought I should tell him.

"If nothing comes back then it will all be wonderful, and if something does come back…well…then we have bigger problems, don't we?"

Jack heaved himself out of the chair. "That's a fair point. I'd better go make a few phone calls before they all go home for the evening. In the meantime, *stay out of this*, Tedi. I mean it."

"Of course, I'll stay out of it. Why would I get involved? I'll let you do your job."

The last thing I even wanted to do was put Kate's name in a search engine. No way. I'd leave it to the professionals.

He leaned down so his hands were braced on my desk. "I mean it. Don't go off half-cocked and talk to Kate Beckswith."

He could be so infuriating.

"I am not going to speak with Kate," I replied through gritted teeth. "Give me credit for a little common sense."

Straightening, he turned toward the door. "I'll call you if I find out anything interesting."

"So no news is good news?"

"Isn't that the usual way?"

It certainly was. I'd never prayed harder for a silent phone.

Chapter Eighteen

SOMEHOW, I ENDED up driving to my dad's house. It wasn't planned, and in fact, I'd specifically told myself that I wasn't going to that part of Ravenmist. I was only planning to get takeout from the Chinese place and that's what I did.

I was starving, and I'd ordered enough for about four people and that's when the whole plan went downhill. I thought about how much my dad liked Chinese takeout and the next thing I knew I was pulling up into his driveway and ringing his doorbell, the smell of chicken and spices teasing my nostrils.

But I wasn't going to bring up the whole Ocala coincidence. Jack was checking Kate out and I was staying out of it, just as I'd agreed to do.

Dad's eyes widened in surprise, but he grinned and beckoned me in. "Pumpkin, what a nice surprise. I didn't know you were stopping by."

Because I hadn't called, which I probably should have in hindsight.

I clutched the large bag of food to my chest. "I'm sorry, Dad. I should have called or something. It was an impulse. I had too much Chinese and I thought about you."

"When one of my beautiful daughters brings me Chinese food, I know she needs to talk." He took the brown paper sack and placed it on the kitchen counter. "Is it Jack, pumpkin?"

What? Jack? Dad thought I wanted to talk about Jack?

"Um, no. He and I are just friends. There's nothing between us."

My dad began unpacking the food while I shrugged out of my coat. It was warm in the house, the fireplace glowing merrily on the far wall. His new condo wasn't big, but it was cozy and comfortable.

"I saw you two dancing at the ball the other night. You looked good together."

"We're just friends," I said firmly, sitting down at the small table. Dad's new place had a great room design; the kitchen was open to the living room with only a tiny table in between to make the transition. "It's not romantic."

"Methinks you doth protest too much," Dad said before popping an egg roll into his mouth and chewing with relish. "Okay, let's say you're not here to talk about Jack. What are you here to talk about then? Because I know when something is bothering my Pumpkin."

Yes, Dad's Pumpkin has had better days than today. I was wishing that I could go back in time and walk right by Doctor Aiken, not talking to her at all. Then I wouldn't be thinking the things that I was thinking now.

"Is it simply life in general?"

Life in general? Why yes, it was.

"You could say that. Maybe it's just the *after the holidays* doldrums."

These egg rolls were good and so was the chicken and broccoli. I ate with growing enthusiasm as I realized I was starving.

"You should turn over the inn to your manager and go on a sunny and warm vacation," my dad replied. "Somewhere tropical with lots of rum. You and Missy could go together."

Could Grim Reapers get time off? I really need to ask her about that.

"I wouldn't mind jetting off to a remote island and turning off my cell phone. That sounds like a piece of heaven."

Dad slapped the table and smiled widely. "Then you should do it. You've had your nose to the grindstone all year. Have a little fun, live a little."

"What about you, Dad? Do you need a vacation?"

He chewed thoughtfully and then answered. "I wouldn't mind one, but I went to California in September for your uncle's wedding."

Uncle Dave's nuptials. His fourth and the women were all getting younger. This one was about my age.

"I doubt that was much of a vacation." My mouth had a mind of its own and I couldn't stop the next words from tumbling out. "We could take a vacation as a family. All of us together."

We'd done that many times before and had even managed to have a good time and not kill each other.

Rubbing his chin, Dad appeared to be struggling with his reply. "Pumpkin, I don't think that's going to happen. Your mom and I are friends, but we don't really want to spend our vacations together anymore."

"Oh. Right. Of course. That makes sense."

"I'm glad you understand."

"So I guess you'd want to go on vacation with Kate?"

It came out more like a question than I meant it to. I'd wanted to sound confident and supportive, but it came out kind of pathetic.

"We haven't discussed it but I'm sure we'd have a good time." He paused for a long moment before continuing. "Don't you like Kate?"

"I do," I replied quickly. "I really do. She seems very nice. A lovely person."

"But," he prompted, his brow raised. "You have reservations."

"It's just happened so fast," I confessed with a long sigh. I wanted to say so much but then again, I didn't want to say anything. I was walking a thin line here. "I'm a little blindsided."

"I've known Kate since I was a teenager," Dad reminded me gently. "It doesn't feel fast to me."

"Maybe you should slow down a little."

I wanted to smack myself in the head. I was saying way too much.

"Pumpkin, I can't live my life to make you more comfortable."

My father was being incredibly patient with me and I was being a jerk.

"I know, I know. It's just…you say you know Kate, but she's been gone a long time. I'm sure she's changed and so have you."

His eyes narrowed, and his cheeks flushed slightly. Sure signs that my dad's famous patience was wearing thin.

"We've both changed, that's true. I think she's become an even more wonderful person. She's kind, funny, smart, and she makes me happy."

How could I possibly argue with that? I wasn't even sure that I wanted to. After all, I only had a hunch. A crazy feeling deep down in my gut that the coincidence meant something. It might not mean anything at all.

Kate Beckswith could end up my stepmother at the rate the relationship was going. I didn't want to upset my dad.

"Then I'm happy for you," I replied firmly. "That's what I want for you."

"And that's what I want for you, too. You know, Jack Garrett seems like a good man."

They simply wouldn't let it go.

"You're beating a dead horse, and I am happy, by the way. Extremely happy. Consider me positively giddy."

That made my dad laugh and he stood to pack up the food and toss the garbage. I helped, and we had it done in two shakes of a lamb's tail as he used to say when I was a kid. When the counters were clean and the leftovers stored in his refrigerator – I refused to take them home – I shrugged into my coat to leave.

I'd shown up uninvited and I probably needed to leave in case I said something I didn't want to.

"You should stay, honey. Kate's coming over and we're going to watch *Lord of the Rings*. From the beginning."

My dad's favorite film series. He liked Harry Potter movies, too.

"That sounds like a several night marathon. I think I'll pass but thank you for the invitation. Why don't you and Kate stop by the inn this weekend and we'll all have lunch?"

"We'd love that. I'll give you call."

Wrapping my scarf around my neck I plunged into the cold, waving to my dad who was standing at the window. Before I could get into my car another vehicle pulled in next to it.

Kate. Literally the last person I wanted to see. I'd promised Jack that I would stay out of it and that's exactly what I wanted to do.

For the most part.

She stepped out of her sedan and greeted me with a smile and a wave. "Tedi, I didn't realize you were going to be here. How lovely."

"I didn't know, either. I had some Chinese food and I stopped by on a whim."

She nodded toward the house. "We're going to watch movies and eat popcorn. You should join us."

"I need to get back to the inn. Lots to do." I hesitated for a moment, remembering what I'd promised Jack, but my mouth was already in gear and my brain hadn't caught up. "Colin

Aiken's wife is a guest at the inn and I want to check on her, see if she needs anything."

"I heard that," Kate said in a soft voice. "It's so sad for Bitty. Losing a loved one is always difficult."

I was already well down the rabbit hole. A different one from last night.

"She mentioned that she and Colin lived in Ocala for awhile. Did you know them, by any chance?"

I held my breath waiting for her answer.

Kate shook her head. "I'm afraid not. Ocala isn't that small. Not like Ravenmist."

I slowly exhaled in relief. Kate hadn't even flinched when I mentioned Doctor Aiken. Not a facial tic, nothing.

"Well, I better get going and let you go inside out of the cold. Enjoy the movie. I mentioned to Dad that maybe you two could stop by this weekend and we'd all have lunch."

Her face lit up and she clapped her gloved hands together. "That sounds amazing. I'd love that."

With another wave to my dad who was now standing in the open doorway of his home, I climbed into my car and backed out of the driveway. My phone began vibrating and I checked it before pulling into traffic. A text from Missy.

You're not home. Where could you be? Come meet me at Daisy's. I have a craving for coconut custard pie.

She was right, I wasn't home. But I wouldn't mind a slice of pie. Next stop The Grateful Raven.

Chapter Nineteen

"I'M THE WORST daughter in the world," I moaned over a giant slice of coconut pie. "The absolute worst. I don't deserve parents."

Daisy patted my hand that wasn't holding a fork. "Now, now, it can't be all that bad. It's only natural that you're having a tough time with this. You're not a terrible daughter. You're a wonderful daughter."

Daisy had closed up The Grateful Raven, pulled the shades on the windows, and let Amelia and Charles come down to visit with Missy and me. The two spirits were zipping happily around the room while Daisy, Missy, and I demolished large amounts of sweets at a corner booth.

"Daisy's right," Missy agreed, digging into her own slice of pie. "You're being too hard on yourself. And I know your parents adore you. They understand that this is a difficult time."

I shoveled another mouthful into my pie hole. "And I'm not making it any easier."

Charles stopped long enough to stand by our table. "Your parents sound nicer than mine. They threatened to disinherit and banish me from the family. My father said my name would never cross their lips again."

Amelia nodded from across the room. "And my father said he was going to send me to stay with relatives."

That did sound bad. My parents had once threatened to pack me in a box and send me to Australia during a strange phase when I was obsessed with kangaroos, but they'd never threatened to erase me from the Hamilton family. If anything, they'd said I'd never be free of them. They'd made it sound like a threat and I'd taken it seriously.

"Why can't I accept Kate? Why can't I be a better person? She seems nice. She makes Dad happy. Why isn't that enough for me?"

"Because you want it to be your mother," Daisy replied patiently. "That's normal, Tedi."

My gaze resting on the two spirits, I shook my head. "The last thing I am is normal."

"So you think it's just a weird coincidence that Colin, his wife, and Kate all lived in Ocala?" Missy asked. "That it's all innocent?"

"You should have seen her face when I mentioned Doctor Aiken. Not a flicker of recognition, not a nose twitch. No reaction. Then she said how sad it must be to lose a loved one. She seemed genuinely sorry for Liz's loss."

"Who's Liz?" Daisy asked, offering more pie. There was no way I could eat another bite. They'd have to roll me out of the front door.

"That's the wife's first name. Well, actually it's Elisabetta but she told me to call her Liz."

Frowning, I replayed my conversation with the doctor from beginning to end. Something…wasn't quite right and I couldn't put my finger on it. It was niggling at the back of my mind and–

Wait. I've got it.

If Kate had never met Doctor Elisabetta Aiken, how on earth did she know her nickname was Bitty? As far as I knew, Liz hadn't told anyone else, but even if she had the name wouldn't have fallen so casually from Kate's lips. That only meant one thing.

Kate had lied. She'd known Liz or Colin or both at some point in the past.

Kate had lied. Lied, lied, lied. Right to my face without a flicker of guilt.

"Tedi, are you listening to me?"

The voice was Missy's and the answer was no. I had no idea what my best friend had just said.

"No, I was thinking about Kate."

"What about her?"

"I think she's lied to me. I think she knew Liz and Colin in Ocala." Missy and Daisy gave me a puzzled look. "She knew Liz's private nickname that Colin had given her. How would she know that?"

"I don't know," Daisy said, her brow knitted in thought. "I can't think of a way that she would know. She said she'd never met the woman, correct?"

"Correct," I replied briskly, my mind already whirling with possibilities. "So that begs the question, what else has she lied about?"

"I think you've missed the bigger picture here," Missy said, grabbing my coat and pushing it toward me. "Your father is all alone with a possible killer. That doesn't bother you?"

I needed to smack myself in the forehead. Repeatedly. But I'd have to do it later. I needed to get to my dad's house as quickly as possible.

Struggling into my coat, I simultaneously dug for my car keys in my purse. "I have to go. What if she's one of those black widow killers that murders every man she's with? My dad could be next, for all we know."

Daisy hopped up from the booth. "I'll drive. You're too upset to be behind the wheel. There's room for all of us in my van."

"Thanks. Let's get out of here."

WE MUST HAVE looked quite the sight to any onlooker on the sidewalk after dark, careening through the streets of Ravenmist like an out-of-control rollercoaster. Townsfolk rarely went much more than five miles an hour over the limit of thirty-five, but currently Daisy had the pedal to the metal. The speedometer read fifty and she was wasn't slowing down for corners. We were being thrown all over the inside of the van. All of us except for

Amelia and Charles, of course. They didn't have a corporeal form to be thrown about.

I wasn't sure why the Young Lovers had joined us, but I hadn't had time to object as Daisy had loaded us into her beloved and ancient VW.

Note to self – don't ever let Jack smell the inside of this vehicle.

"He's not answering," Missy said, her voice climbing higher as Daisy took another corner on two wheels.

"Leave a message," I replied, holding onto the door handle for dear life. "I can't believe this is the one time he doesn't answer."

Missy had her cell phone pressed to her ear trying to get in touch with Jack. I needed to talk to him about Kate and what I'd figured out. Normally, he answered right away but he would pick this particular moment to go missing. My dad's life could be on the line here.

"Should we call 911?" Daisy asked from the driver's seat.

"No, because it really isn't an emergency. Not a real one, anyway."

I couldn't tell Delores the emergency operator that I had a *gut feeling* that Kate was a killer.

"This is fun," Amelia said from the back seat, a big smile on her face. Charles was grinning as well and holding her hand. At least they were happy.

When Daisy drove into my dad's driveway, she was going so fast she almost rear-ended Kate's car, stopping mere inches from the bumper. We all tumbled out of the vehicle, falling over each other. The Young Lovers stayed seated, content to watch from a distance. I hiked my purse on my shoulder, determined to stomp up the front porch steps and...

Do what? I didn't exactly know but I was sure that Kate and my dad shouldn't be by themselves. I had my foot on the bottom step when Jack's official SUV pulled in front of the house and he climbed out. He was wearing his uniform and a serious expression. He walked right up to me and placed his hand on my shoulder.

"Not now, Tedi. I have business here and I'm going to have to ask you to step aside."

"Business?" I parroted, still shocked to see him. "We've been trying to call you."

"I'm on duty. Now if you will step aside?"

This was the all-business Sheriff Jack Garrett. He'd barely given me a glance, his gaze trained on the front door.

"Jack? I'm here because—"

"I know why you're here and after you promised me you wouldn't interfere. Now go home, Tedi. I'll take care of this."

His voice was gruff, and I had a feeling I wasn't his favorite person at the moment. I could explain if he let me. Instead, the door opened and the porch light came on, bright and almost blinding. My dad and Kate stepped out, curious as to what was going on in the front yard and wondering about all the headlights.

"Sheriff," my dad greeted Jack with a smile and a wave. "Is

everything okay? Tedi, are you alright?"

My gaze traveled back and forth from Jack to Kate. His expression never changed but hers did. There was a moment when her features turned from happy to…resigned. So it wasn't a shock when she spoke up before Jack or I could answer.

"The sheriff is here to see me, Dan. Aren't you, Sheriff?"

"Yes, ma'am." Jack nodded, taking a step back so that there was a pathway for Kate to walk between himself and I. "May I escort you to the station, Mrs. Beckswith?"

"I'll get my coat and purse. Dan, I'll call you tomorrow, okay?"

My dad nodded and helped her on with her coat, giving her a hug and a kiss on the cheek before she descended the steps. I watched my dad as he watched her get in Jack's car and drive away.

This sucked. I couldn't think of a worse moment for him that I'd personally witnessed. He'd aged before my eyes and that happy-go-lucky man had disappeared. He had to know that this situation wasn't good. Far from it.

"I'm going to stay here. You guys can go ahead home. Thanks for the ride, Daisy."

Climbing the steps, I stepped in front of my dad and wrapped my arms around his waist like I had when I was a kid and too short to give him a proper hug. At first, he simply stood there and then his arms embraced me, the hold tightening with each passing second.

"You don't have to stay, pumpkin. I'm okay."

"There isn't any place I'd rather be, Dad. You can't get rid of me. Let's go watch *Lord of the Rings.*"

He pulled back and our gazes met. "I think that's a great idea. Your friends are welcome to join us."

Even the ghosts? That might not be a great idea. Daisy and Missy must have agreed because they were climbing into the van and waving goodbye before I could ask them to stay. Dad and I watched until their red taillights disappeared into the night.

"How about some popcorn? Are you hungry?"

After all of that pie? Absolutely not.

"Sounds great. Why don't you start the movie and I'll make it?"

There wasn't anything I wouldn't do for my father. Even puke later.

Chapter Twenty

A WEEK LATER Ravenmist was beginning to get back to normal. It had been big news when Kate had been called in for questioning in the death of Colin Aiken. Jack's law enforcement contacts had come up with the connection quite quickly. Kate's husband and Aiken had been in a business deal together.

Her subsequent confession and arrest had the town talking but it had petered out eventually. There wasn't much drama, really. No car chase. No wild accusations. No standoff at the OK Corral. Just a sad, middle-aged woman who had quietly told her story to Jack, holding nothing back. I'd assumed Kate was a woman scorned but that was far from the truth.

Sitting at a window booth in The Grateful Raven, I watched as the county officer escorted a handcuffed Kate – with Jack right behind – out of the station. She was being transferred to the county lockup as Ravenmist didn't have the adequate accommodations to hold her until her date with the judge. Jack said something to the cop and then to Kate before she climbed into the back of the vehicle. He stood there watching the squad car drive away before turning around, our gazes meeting through the window.

I assumed he'd return to the station but instead he entered the restaurant and slid into the booth across from me.

"I haven't talked to you in awhile."

That was true. He'd been busy, and I hadn't wanted to bother him. I had a feeling that eventually he'd come back around for a slice of pie or a steak sandwich.

"It looked like you had your hands full," I replied, taking a sip of my coffee. "I think the whole town has given you a wide berth. You've had a scowl on your face for days. For a man that solved a murder, you haven't been too happy about it."

He studied his hands for a long moment, then looked up. I could see the confusion in his eyes and was surprised by it. Jack was a man who saw life in black and white, no shades of gray.

"I kind of wish I hadn't," he finally said. "Kate Beckswith has had some lousy luck thanks to Colin Aiken. But she took a life and she'll have to pay for that."

I couldn't argue. Kate had been dealt a lousy hand. Far from being broken-hearted, Kate had barely known Colin Aiken. But her husband had. Somehow Colin had convinced Kate's husband to go into a shady, get rich quick business venture with him. It was bad news all around. It was a sham and a fraud like most of Colin's businesses and Kate and her husband had ended losing their life savings. They'd had to sell the horse farm and the stress had basically killed him. He'd had a heart attack not long after and passed away. Kate had come back to Ravenmist for revenge. As far as she was concerned, she'd had nothing to lose.

She'd already lost it all.

"Does she regret it?" I asked softly. "If she shows remorse, the judge–"

"No," Jack interrupted, a muscle moving in his jaw. "She doesn't regret it. She said she'd do it again. Anything for her beloved Jim. She's not even scared to go to prison. She said that she's already been there since he died."

"I think she underestimates how lousy prison is going to be."

"I do too, but she made her choices. We can't change that. Maybe the judge will have mercy for her when she tells her story."

"At the trial?"

He sighed and leaned back in the booth. "There isn't going to be a trial. She's going to plead guilty. She doesn't want to drag this out. She wants it to be all over. That's why she confessed."

I'd read the stories in the local paper. Kate had slipped the bow and arrow out of the party when no one was looking, and the lights were down for a slow song. Then she'd followed Aiken outside, shooting him from a spot between two trees. She'd left him outside to be found, which of course Jack and I did a few hours later.

"He never saw it coming."

Jack frowned. "We don't know that for sure. She said she found him outside and took him by surprise."

Except that I did know that Colin never saw it coming. The last thing he'd remembered was Daisy. But Jack didn't know that, and I was never going to tell him.

"How's your dad?"

"He's good," I replied. "At least he's going to be. He's sad, of course, and feels betrayed. He thought he knew her because they'd dated in high school. He thought she was the same."

"Life changed her. Have you been spending much time with him?"

"Every day. I assume he'll tell me to get lost when he gets tired of me."

Jack chuckled and signaled the waitress for a cup of coffee. "You're not too bad of company. When you're not being annoying, that is."

"Did you hear the one about the pot and the kettle?"

"Can't say as I have." The waitress slid his steaming cup in front of him just as the diner door opened and my dad and Doctor Liz Aiken walked in. Together. They sat down in a corner booth.

This was an…interesting development.

"They have a lot in common," Jack observed. "They could both do worse."

"Do you think – No. It's probably just – No."

I couldn't even begin to process the idea. Liz Aiken and my dad.

"She's probably just giving him medical advice."

"Uh huh. Sure, that's it." Jack pulled a twenty-dollar bill from his pocket. "I've got twenty bucks that says your dad is going to take a spring break vacation in Miami in the near future."

The way my dad and Liz were talking so intently, their heads close together, I had the distinct feeling I'd lose that bet.

"I'll pass, Jack. Your last twenty dollars is still safe with me."

He nodded toward the kitchen door. "You know Daisy's visiting family could use a Miami vacation. They're awfully pale. They should get outside more."

I followed his gaze to where Amelia and Charles were peeking out of the swinging door. Holy moly, Jack didn't have a clue that they were ghosts. Since coming to Daisy's, they seemed to have gained a great deal more energy and looked almost alive and kicking. I really needed to talk to that Madame Harriet or whatever her name was.

Something weird was definitely going on in this town.

It was just another day in Ravenmist.

I hope you enjoyed Ghoul You Be My Valentine! There will be more in the Ravenmist Whodunit series coming soon.

Thank you for reading.

Don't miss a thing! Sign up to be notified of Olivia's new releases:

Mailing List

http://eepurl.com/gdVe3T

About The Author

Olivia Jaymes is a wife, mother, lover of sexy romance and cozy mysteries, and caffeine addict. She lives with her husband, son, and two spoiled dogs in central Florida and spends her days typing on her computer with a canine on her lap.

She is currently working on a new cozy mystery series – *A Ravenmist Whodunit* – in addition to her other ongoing romance series.

Visit Olivia Jaymes at

www.OliviaJaymes.com